A RAVEN'S DREAM

STARSIDE SAGA #2

ERIC KENT EDSTROM

UNDERMOUNTAIN**BOOKS**

To J

1

DIE, RAVEN, DIE

No one saw the raven flutter and alight upon the windowsill in the Citadel tower. So no one crossed her fingers and said three times, "Die, raven, die." No one saw the delicate hand offer the bird a corner of bread. No one heard what was said.

No one witnessed any of this, yet uneasiness seeped into hearts of all who lived in Starside. Chills crept across people's bodies, and forebodings thrummed upon the unseen world of the mercusine.

The raven swallowed its morsel and took flight.

Beneath the Citadel lay the Divide, the great and impervious wall separating Starside from Moonside. The Divide was a monolith of seamless black stone marching seven miles to the harbor and then another five into the Ansin Ocean.

Moonside huddled unseen beneath its ever-present

blanket of fog. What transpired there was known only to the dead—and to Her Enlightened Majesty.

But the tiled roofs and creamy-sided buildings of Starside shone in the last rays of daylight. The magnificent city spread wide beneath the raven, tumbling in tiers downslope toward the sea. The air was clear, the evening crisp. A sliver of moon rose to the east.

The raven soared along the Divide, carried by cold mountain breezes. It banked left and dove toward a bell tower thrusting heavenward.

The dire feeling faded from people's awareness, whether they abided in Gristenside greathouses or in Cheapsgate shacks. In all places, the superstitious tapped their ears and whispered, "Til protect me." Some reached for a cup of trezz, some merely shivered and went on with their chores.

The bird's wings hissed through the air as it passed an opening atop the bell tower. The girl who stood there didn't see it or hear its warning squawk. So she didn't cross her fingers and say three times, "Die, raven, die."

Her bare feet pressed the rough plank floor. Her cat sat nearby, tail curled around its small white feet.

Kila Sigh shivered and rubbed her arms. Only once before had she come so close to the Citadel, the great home of Her Enlightened Majesty. It was—as her brother Wen had repeatedly warned her—stupid to risk it. The farther one ventured uphill from the stinking docks and slums of Cheapsgate, the richer the neighborhoods. Here, beneath the Citadel, people were very wealthy indeed.

But Kila wasn't here to rob anyone. Not today.

Can we go home now? Nax sent to her. The voice of her cat came directly into her mind. Three weeks had passed since the little gray cat with the white chin and socks had bonded to her. Kila still found the experience eerie, but she could not imagine life without it.

I'm not finished, Kila sent back. She hadn't even started.

You've been standing here forever.

Cats had no sense of time. It had been a quarter of an hour. At most. *Take a nap,* Kila sent, irritated by the distraction. She needed to concentrate.

She and her feline friend had sneaked into the bell tower and climbed its winding staircase so she could get to this vantage point overlooking Gristenside. She wasn't *supposed* to be there, but she needed the view for what she was about to attempt.

The tower was open on four sides here, allowing a breeze to waft through. A one-ton brass bell hung in the shadows behind Kila, etched with a scene from the Theb. She hadn't stopped to study it. Kila did not believe in the gods.

What are you trying to do? Nax sent. There was more impatience than curiosity in the question. A feeling of boredom accompanied the cat's sending, making Kila's arms and legs feel heavy.

I'm looking.

For what?

For whatever I can see. Now hush.

Kila slowed her breathing, counting the in and out breaths to avoid thinking about anything else. This exercise was supposed to help her access her mercus vision.

So far, the vision had only come to her when things were dangerous and her heart was pounding. At first, Wen hadn't believed her stories about the vision, about how she could see metal objects hidden inside pockets or through walls. Once convinced, he'd pressed her to master the skill. Such an ability offered obvious advantages for a thief.

So here she was. To practice. And she had better succeed, because coin was running low and Wen needed another batch of Finta Sahng's medicine.

The sun was sinking behind the mountains that backed the Citadel. The massive wedge-shaped fortress thrust from the mountains like the prow of a great ship, narrowing to merge into the Divide. It was said Her Enlightened Majesty sometimes strolled along the Divide, the only place she was allowed to venture without her Fell Guard in attendance. The central tower soared upward, windows lit from within by mercus lights.

To Kila it seemed a cold and foreboding place. Much better to live in Gristenside, in a warm mansion surrounded by family. Her Enlightened had nobody.

The odd mood that had passed over her before

returned, and she shivered again. Her breathing exercise was not working.

Are you seeing something? Nax asked. She had stretched herself in a fading patch of sunlight. The tip of her tail flicked with impatience.

Kila gave up counting breaths. It was a boring waste of time. Besides, it took her in the wrong direction. Usually when the mercus vision happened, it was preceded by a feeling she called the "zing." The word described how her body felt when it happened. The world came to her with such clarity. Every sight, smell, and sound sharpened. The texture of all she touched more finely detailed.

The only thing that reliably brought the zing into Kila's body was danger. That's what she needed now.

She bounced on her toes and swung her arms. The bell tower offered a unique opportunity to scare her witless, which was just the thing she needed.

The north side of the tower faced the Divide. Running parallel to it was the Starside wall. Its top was just above the bell tower and no more than three hundred paces away. There were no Watch patrols up there now, so no one would see her.

On the south side was a small plaza surrounded by shops serving the Radiant families of Gristenside. Directly below her were the Baths of Ori, a compound dedicated to the followers of the goddess. A rectangular pool steamed in the evening glow. Near to it stood the domed temple where the public could seek the assistance of the Sensuals.

Nobody was out and about at the moment, the stores having already closed for the day. Dinner would be steaming on plates around the quarter soon.

Kila leaned farther out and craned her neck to look up—toward the bell tower roof. The eaves overhung a little bit. But not so much that she could easily reach. The mortar between bricks had eroded in a few places, offering nice finger-holds. A low, white railing provided a step.

Thinking too long about stunts always made them more dangerous. So she stepped onto the railing, turned, and jammed her fingertips into the shallow gaps in the brickwork. She hung there, one foot on the railing, fingers of her right hand dug in.

She didn't look down. But just the thought of the drop below her toes sent a wave of nervous heat washing over her. She spotted a protrusion of brick trim-work above the opening.

She pushed off with her toes, pulled with her fingers, and reached with the other hand.

Got it. She found a crevice for one toe, enough to let her firm up her finger grip on the trim-work. Her palms grew clammy as the distance below her pulled at her mind.

What are you doing? Nax asked.

I'm going onto the roof.

I want to come.

Hanging a hundred paces over empty air by her fingertips, Kila wasn't exactly in a position to pick up the cat. *Maybe next time.*

Hold still, Nax sent.

Kila realized what the cat was going to do. *Nax! No, wait!*

Too late. The cat leapt to the railing, then onto Kila's dangling leg. Claws stabbed into Kila's calf, thigh, buttocks, waist, back, shoulder, and scalp as the small gray cat scaled her like a tree trunk. And then the weight of the little beastie left her entirely.

Gritting her teeth to hold on while her body flared from fiery scratches, Kila looked up. All she could see was the little gray's hind legs and tail. *You flea bag! You Kil-lickin' tangleball!*

Nax turned to look down at her. *Come up. The view is interesting.*

Still swearing under her breath, Kila released a hand and found the edge of the roof. A moment suspended, dangling by one hand, then her other hand found purchase. Hefting and grunting, she worked her way onto the roof.

She blew out a long breath, and a nervous chuckle came out unbidden. *That was stupid even for me.*

I thought the same thing.

The conical roof sloped gently upward. A thick staff protruded from the central peak, a gold-plated circle mounted on the top. The symbol of Ori. Kila planted herself on the roof, one arm hooked around the post to keep herself in place.

The view was grand. And nobody would see her here. Not unless Her Enlightened came out to the tip of the Citadel. Even then she'd need a spyglass.

Nax nosed around the roof, walking to the very edge and thrusting her face over. Kila knew the cat was sure-footed enough not to fall, but her stomach lurched just watching.

That feeling was exactly what she was hoping for. And now that she was up here, she knew she'd eventually have to go back down. Thinking about it made her heart thump faster. Good. Descending was more gut-clenching because you *had* to look down to find your footing.

And then it happened. The zing arose, sending chills across her scalp. The smell of chimney smoke hit her nose. The call of a distant raven came to her ears. She looked for it down the length of the Divide, but the only birds in sight were gulls.

The view was fantastic. The entire city spread before her, from the Citadel to the merchants' quarter of Terriside. The main thoroughfare of the city, the Street of Sorrows, wended its way in long switchbacks down toward the docks. Far away, the empty ruins of the Blasted Quarter skirted along the southern stretch of the outer wall. The buildings there were crumbled messes, many with walls missing, exposing empty chambers within. To the east, beyond the city wall, lay the smoky slums of Cheapsgate bordering the docks. Ships were moored there with bare masts, while farther out, one of Her Enlightened Majesty's ships patrolled the mouth of Brintso Bay.

Five miles to sea, the massive Sea Bastion hunkered at the end of the Divide like a shining white boulder, its thousand-foot flashtower thrusting toward the clouds. From Kila's perch it was a vague shape, lost in haze and the growing darkness.

Kila slid her fingers over the wooden shingles beneath her, feeling the ridges of the grain. She smelled something rotting beneath the shingles, like damp leaves. The zing passed over her like a wave. Her arms prickled and chilled.

Now she would try the mercus vision.

As far as she could tell, the mercus vision required her to relax her eyesight. Not let it go out of focus, but instead to let her eyes see the world without naming anything in it. The roof was no longer a roof. The shingles were no longer shingles. The Divide and the Citadel were not what they were called. They just were. Only the unnamed world could reveal what she wanted to see.

Metal. Preferably gold and silver.

And then it happened.

The pole she had her arm hooked around began to glow with a reddish light. Iron.

The circle of Ori glowed a bright gray. Steel.

The circle also shed an orange-yellow haze. Gold. From the thin coat of leafing.

These glows didn't shed light onto anything. They were auras in Kila's vision of the unnamed, not lights in the world of the named.

She turned her attention to the Starside wall just beneath the Divide. Sharp and tiny lines showed her where whale oil lanterns were mounted on iron posts along its top. Below her, more red glows showed sewer grates, wrought iron fences, and garden gates.

The brass bell beneath her glowed greenish-yellow and was so big she felt it throbbing through her bones, as if it were ringing.

She turned her eyes to the Pinnacle atop the Citadel tower. Silver and nickel. She could not imagine why so much silver would be put to such a useless purpose. That was rich folk for you.

She looked to Gristenside. Drain gutters glowed the reddish-orange of tin alloyed with copper. These gutters lined the roofs of all the magnificent houses there. She wondered how many copper coins could be made from the downspouts alone.

It's working, she sent to Nax. *I see metal. Everywhere.*

You could have found metal in the Warren.

Kila wasn't sure if Nax was missing the point on purpose or if she was just trying to get a rise out of Kila. Cats could get surly when bored.

I'm looking for things to steal, she sent. It was better for them both if Kila was direct.

Oh. Good idea.

And that was that. Nax was satisfied. So much so, she climbed onto Kila's shoulder and nudged her with her soft face. Kila scratched Nax between the ears and kept studying the city.

Most of the metal she saw would be obvious without the mercus vision. Nobody would bother stealing lamp posts or iron fences anyway.

She chose one home nearby. It had cedar shingles and brickwork walls coated over with the creamy white pargo common to the city. Deep blue storm shutters were hooked open.

A wrought iron hand rail climbed the front steps to the entry. Brass knocker on the door. More alloy gutters lined the roof.

On an out breath, Kila relaxed her vision further. Tiny sparks showed her the latches on the windows. Good. Those were inside the house. Even if she had a spyglass, she wouldn't be able to see them from where she sat. But the mercus showed the glows and sparks of the latches clearly.

"Show me more," she said to herself. The metals glowed in her vision. There had to be much more of it inside the house.

A hazy brass shape hung beyond a second-floor window. Kila thought it was a lantern. A wall sconce, perhaps.

But that was it. Nothing more came to her. The

metals were too far away, or they were behind too much other material.

How am I going to get down? Nax sent.

Kila let the mercus vision go and regarded the little gray. *You should have thought of that before climbing up my body. You do see that, don't you?*

No.

Kila couldn't help but laugh. Nax was smart in so many ways, but there were blind spots in her thinking. She couldn't count or even comprehend numbers above four. She had little sense of time or distance. And clearly, she wasn't great at planning ahead.

What are *you, Naxie?* she sent, fondly stroking the cat's short, soft fur. She had asked this question dozens of times since bonding with the cat.

Nax lifted her face and squinted at Kila. *I'm a cat.*

What do you talk to the other cats about?

We don't talk. Nax's agitation with the tedious questions came as heat prickling across Kila's scalp.

You never say anything to them?

We know each other's minds. The cat hopped down from Kila's shoulder and stretched. *Get me down from here.*

Kila considered the odd statement. Nax had emphasized the word "know", as if "knowing" was something they did to each other. *You share thoughts without words?*

I suppose.

Kila could tell Nax was getting bored with the

conversation. Cats did not like talking about things they didn't understand.

Are you a demayne? she asked.

I don't think so.

So you're saying you could *be a demayne?*

The Donse Masters of the Way of Til claimed cats were possessed by evil spirits called demayne. That's why the Donse Masters killed every cat they could get their hands on. Hence the two-gold-skillet bounty they paid for every cat.

Nax answered with an irritable meow.

Kila laughed and said aloud, "Let's get down from this tower and find some trouble to get in to. Hop on."

Holding onto the iron pole, Kila took one more look around. The sun had sunk beyond the mountains, leaving their peaks silhouetted against a darkening sky. Night would soon cover the city, just as Kila liked it.

How are we getting down? Nax asked.

Very carefully.

Good idea.

2

A GREAT HUNGER

The Hargothe sat up in his bed, withered body propped against thick down cushions. His empty eye sockets itched from keeping his eyelids open so long. But he knew they unsettled those who sought his audience.

Few ever descended to his quiet crypt beneath the Cathedral of Til. Partly out of respect for his need to protect his keen senses from too much stimulation. But also because he terrified them.

The Hargothe enjoyed their fear, which he felt as dissonant thrums along the mercusine threads permeating this and all worlds. As the Hargothe, he was especially attuned to the subtle world of power known as the mercus. Some Donse Masters had greater skill at setting candles alight and moving needles with their power, but only the Hargothe could project his thoughts through the mercusine and touch another person's mind.

He lowered his eyelids and licked his papery lips. "Where is the girl?"

The girl. He had felt her awakening to the mercus. He longed to bring her into this chamber. With proximity, many things became possible that he could not do at a distance.

"We believe she is in the Cheapsgate slums, Seer Hargothe," said Highest Chilow. The man had been Til's Highest in this city for twenty years. His voice didn't quaver, but there was anxiety in it. He knew well what the Hargothe could do. "The girl is elusive as smoke in shadow, but a reliable source claims she still lives in the Warren."

"Then why haven't you collected her?" The Hargothe's voice never rose above a whisper, lest he start coughing. He lifted a hand and scratched a thick fingernail along a scab on the side of his nose. Flakes of skin fell away.

"If I may ask, of what use is a Cheapsgate waif to us?"

"She has awakened to the mercus. Powerfully so."

Dunne Chilow swallowed, a disgusting, wet sound that grated in the Hargothe's ears. "But should not a girl go to the Spinsters or Sensuals?"

"And cede her power to those crones and harlots?" the Hargothe said. "This girl's potential is too great to squander. Those who serve the handmaiden goddesses grow too bold as it is. They should bow to you, Highest Chilow. Instead they flout the law and increase their power."

Strictly speaking, this was heresy. The segregation of the genders was prescribed in the Theb. In that holy text Til directed men to the Way of Til, and women to the orders of the lesser goddesses, Ori and Pol. That was as it should be. But for three generations, Ori's harlots had been seducing men of mercusine potential to join their order, depriving Til his due.

Her Enlightened Majesty—whose mind was clouded by the harlots' lies—refused to order the Watch to drag those men from the Baths of Ori and into the Abbey where they belonged. So it only made sense for the Way of Til to apprehend women of mercusine potential. For Til's glory, all is permitted.

The Hargothe said, "Rest easy, Highest Chilow. We shan't teach her to read, or any such nonsense. In fact, she need never be seen. Bring her to me and I'll put her talents to good use, glorifying Til."

Highest Chilow's breath whistled in his nostrils, betraying the tension in him. He disagreed, but not enough to contradict the Hargothe. A stale smell came from the man. His gut gurgled from the anxiety of facing the only man more powerful than he was.

How it must rankle, to achieve the highest seat in the Way and find yourself under the thumb of a blind invalid lying in a crypt. The Hargothe's title did not confer authority. The Hargothe's power did.

It was the threat of what the Hargothe could do that checked Highest Chilow now. He had witnessed the tortures the Seer inflicted on his victims. Without moving a finger the Hargothe could bring a man to the floor, writhing in such exquisite agony he begged for death.

The Hargothe allowed Highest Chilow to stew in discomfort a while longer before continuing. "There are many greedy palms in Cheapsgate," he said. "Employ an agent who speaks the Cheaps patois to bribe the Warren's master. I must have that girl. Surely the harlots have felt her upon the mercusine. They seek her, too, have no doubt about that."

"Yes, Seer Hargothe."

"See to it your agents do not harm the girl more than necessary. I need her mind alert."

"Yes, Seer Hargothe. Is there aught else I can do for you?"

"Leave."

The Highest and his accompanying Donse Masters shuffled from his chamber. The stench of their sweat lingered, making the Hargothe's nose crinkle.

He calmed himself and sank into the mercusine, feeling for the girl. She had become a flavor to him, easily recognized. Each taste richer than the last. But she wasn't upon the mercusine at the moment. Pity.

He had tried to capture her himself. But being carried about the city on a sedan chair had been too much for his frail body. The streets had overwhelmed him with noise and stink. He'd almost collected her despite that. So close.

But she had been accompanied by spark spirits. The Beloveds of Kil, demayne of other worlds, come here to possess vermin cats. She had bonded one, the Hargothe knew. That was as dangerous as it was vile.

Frustrating. But intriguing, too. The bond between girl and animal proved there were pathways to greater powers. Powers he'd sought his entire life. But first he had to have the girl in chains. Then he could break her at his leisure. Just thinking about it enlivened a great hunger in him.

He rang his bell, wincing to hear the piercing tone. His elderly servant came in. He was a mere acolyte, though older than the Hargothe by a decade. The man was weak in the mercus, which suited the Hargothe well. He needed those close to him to be silent on the subtle levels of the world as well as the gross.

The Hargothe struggled to speak. "Bring one."

A slight intake of breath betrayed the servant's surprise. He quickly masked it. "Yes, Seer."

No matter how deeply the Hargothe drew upon the mercusine, it did little to strengthen his body. For that, he needed sustenance of a different kind.

It seemed an age passed before the old acolyte

returned. Two others flanked a boy. The lad had been prepared well, the stink of the streets washed from him, clean robes put on his back. The Hargothe tasted the boy's sour breath in the air.

If this were Kila Sigh, the Hargothe would prolong the feeding. Perhaps she could give him decades of service, as powerful as she was. But this boy possessed only the faintest spark of mercus.

"The letter to his parents?"

"Prepared, Seer Hargothe."

Through their tears, they would read of their son's great sacrifice in the service of Til. They would learn that he had contracted a dire sickness while helping share Til's word with the wretched of the city. His death would bring them honor. And the ten gold skillets included with the letter would help them accept the lie.

"Bring him closer," the Hargothe said.

The acolytes urged the boy forward. The elderly servant lifted the Hargothe's right hand and placed it on the boy's head. He then fitted beeswax plugs into the Hargothe's ears.

The other acolytes surreptitiously wedged plugs in their ears, too. Wise for them to do so. For the seer immediately plunged his mercus powers into the boy's mind like a soldier driving a spear into an enemy's eye socket.

The boy's scream pierced the Hargothe's wax

plugs, but he strove deeper despite the pain. His fingernails dug into the young scalp even as his powers probed for the tiny spark that connected the boy to the mercusine.

The screams continued until the boy's voice failed and only tortured whispers rasped from his throat.

3

VOLUPTUARY

The Voluptuary of Ori climbed from the copper tub, allowing a Sensual to enfold her in a soft towel. One of the many privileges of her station was a private bath in her quarters. Unfortunately, her moment of relaxation had been disrupted by an odd chill.

A foreboding.

And then something—someone—sparked aflame upon the mercusine. Someone very close by. "Never mind dressing me," she said to her attendant. "Go fetch Yiqa. Quickly now."

The Sensual swished away, multi-colored robes fluttering in her haste. The Voluptuary kept calm. That was her great skill, and why she'd risen to her post at the young age of seventy.

Plucking up another towel from a wicker basket, she commenced patting her hair dry. Her mercusenhanced senses warned of Yiqa's approach, so she was robed and ready to receive the woman by the time she reached the door.

Without greeting, the Voluptuary said, "I have a request."

"Merely ssspeak it," the Alnassi woman said in her odd accent.

"Someone was atop the bell tower just now. I do not think it was a novitiate. Please find her and bring her to me. It's a matter of extreme urgency."

Yiqa bowed and departed, oozing into the hallway like smoke.

Whoever had been testing the mercus, she had made it tremble like an earthquake. Surely Goolsoy had felt it, too.

She smelled him before he arrived. Not a bad stench, just a familiar masculine smell mixed with the tea he always seemed to spill onto his robes.

"You feel?" he said, barging in without a knock. His great beard practically trembled with his excitement.

"I felt it. Yiqa will fetch her."

The man rubbed his thick hands together and nodded gravely. He couldn't keep the smile from his mouth. "So powerful. So *much*."

Enthusiasm may be called for, but not until this new mercus-user was securely ensconced in the novitiates' ward. Until then, there was great danger. If the girl fell into the wrong hands . . . but that would not be tolerated.

Goolsoy said, "I not feel such since—"

"Do not speak of it." The Voluptuary was not a superstitious woman, but she had grown up among simple folk who clung to old fears. Habits of childhood were hard to shed. In this case, there would be no harm in caution. She flicked her fingers behind her back, the ancient ward of blocking the mischief of Pol, goddess of luck.

Goolsoy clamped his mouth shut and started to pace.

The Voluptuary sent him away, lest he drive her mad with his impatience.

She settled into a thickly padded chair, a blanket over her knees. She cupped her hands and plunged into her meditation. The mercusine revealed itself to her. She did not push into it, but merely received.

The mercus showed her many sparks nearby. Goolsoy stood out like a beacon. She let these sparks slip away from her awareness. She need follow only one, distinctive and clear. Yiqa.

The woman did not have mercus powers. But the Voluptuary had marked her, allowing her to track the woman's movements. The mark gave her another, more useful, ability as well.

It would take all of the Voluptuary's powers to use it.

4
THE UNNAMED WORLD

Nax slowly got over the trauma of descending from the bell tower roof. Kila was surprised by how angry the cat had been. Apparently, cats remained fearless of heights only if they were in charge of how they jumped down from them.

Now the two of them ran easily along the roofway, descending the terraced slopes of the Terriside Quarter. They went roof to roof, leaping alleys.

Where are we going? Nax asked.

Kila didn't have a plan. Mostly, she ran for the thrill of it. She especially loved the long falls that landed her on the burlap pads stuffed with straw and rags. Building owners kept them nicely plump, and in return Kila dropped a copper plug into their toll pails.

She marked her coppers so building owners knew she'd paid. Some who used the roofway did not pay.

They always ended up face down, a flickbow bolt in the back.

The roofway let her move about the city quickly, ignoring the twisting streets and taking more direct routes. It also kept her out of the reach of the Watch.

They knew about the roofway. They hated it. But patrolling the rooftops while wearing their heavy armor made them too slow to catch Kila.

Nax liked to run some of the time, but she had to ride along for the longer jumps. Kila was coming to one now, a ten-pace gap from a cooper's workshop, across Ricard's Lane, to the lower roof of a glass blower's.

Kila slowed momentarily so Nax could climb aboard and squirm into the crook of her arm.

Leaning into a sprint, Kila charged to the edge and launched herself into emptiness. Legs wheeling, she let out a whoop and watched the burlap landing pad approach. Her feet struck down, knees bent to absorb some of the impact. She rolled, keeping Nax tightly protected in her arms.

The pair's mastery of this maneuver brought thrills of joy to Kila. They were of one mind.

Kila set Nax back on her feet even as she rolled onto her own. Without a pause in their forward motion, they continued on their way.

Their movements flowed one into the other, the same as breath flowed into breath. Sometimes the flush of vigor grew so great Kila felt the two of them might run forever, above the world, light and free as birds.

The zing from the bell tower had never left her. Though it wasn't as intense as it had been atop the tower, she could hear and see and feel so much more than usual.

It gave her an idea. Her run had taken her to the middle level of Terriside, which descended in three tiers. She was nearing Chance's Corner at a bend in the Street of Sorrows. The main thoroughfare started at the Cheaps, the gate through the city wall that kept the swarms of unclean waifs like Kila from disturbing the respectable citizens of Starside inside the wall. It switchbacked several times as it climbed, the paving stones improving in condition and cleanliness the closer one got to the Citadel.

Kila stopped on the roof of a stationer's shop. The spot offered a clear view of Chance's Corner. The shops were all closed up for the night.

Why did we stop? Nax sent.

I want to try to see metal again.

Nax's breath pulsed in and out of her body like a bellows. Running long distances was not natural for cats. Or so Nax always said.

I'm going to find some water, Nax sent. She didn't wait for Kila to say yes or no. Nax might be Kila's cat, but it didn't mean Nax would do what Kila said. She often did, but not always.

That suited Kila fine. She could sense where Nax was anyway. *Stay in the shadows.*

No response. Nax knew she was on dangerous ground. If anyone got their hands on her, she'd get sacked up and carried off to the Abbey before Kila could click her tongue.

Kila turned her eyes to the street. The people of Terriside did not stay out after dark unless they had urgent business. Those who did venture out at night were smart enough to go out in groups. Mostly. Inevitably, one or two would make their way home alone, drunk.

These were Kila's favorite marks. They were easy to rob and they didn't fight back very skillfully.

She relaxed her vision, trying to recapture the feeling she'd had on the bell tower. The zing was still with her, but at the moment it offered only a slightly heightened sensory awareness.

She shook out her arms and legs, bent her neck side to side to loosen up.

Again, she tried to relax her vision, to not name anything she saw. There was no street, no stones, no buildings, just shapes. That wasn't a man down there, just a moving form. The sounds she heard were not the squawk of a gull or the slam of storm shutters. They were merely sounds.

The smell of smoke, of baking bread, of cooking meat, of atlen droppings. Those had no names. They were mere sensations, neither good nor bad.

Yes. That was it. She felt it now.

The unnamed world came to her while she remained passive and relaxed. And yet she was also alert and ready to move. The contradiction made perfect sense in the moment.

The metals of the world came alight. All the posts, fences, hinges, sewer grates, and roof drain gutters began to glow.

She studied a lone man walking along the street. Yellow glows told of brass buttons. A brass belt buckle. He carried a small folding knife in his pants pocket.

And coins. A purse full of silver and copper plugs. She couldn't count them from here. That could wait until she had them in her hands.

Someone comes, Nax sent.

The mercus vision vanished, leaving the world stark and ordinary.

What?

Someone comes toward you. They have the manner of a sneak.

Can you show me?

Kila and Nax had tried to share each other's vision before, but the results had been fleeting and confusing.

No time. Run. There was more in Nax's sending than the words. It contained all the urgency of a nightmare, of the horrific feeling of being chased by something unstoppable and impossibly strong.

Kila ran.

5

WORLD WENT WHITE

here are you? Kila sent as she leapt across a narrow alley.

On a roof.

Stay there.

Kila dodged around a chimney and chanced a look over her shoulder. She didn't see anyone behind her, but the sense of being chased slithered up and down her spine. She didn't know how much of that feeling came from Nax and how much was her own instinct.

She angled across a row of homes with gritty ceramic tile roofs. The curved tops of the tiles made the footing tricky. Good. Maybe that would slow her pursuer, whoever it was.

A twist in the Street of Sorrows approached straight ahead. Much too broad to jump. She'd have to drop to the street. Only two places to do that in this area. The first was a stack of wooden crates next to the

Harvin Inn. The other required her to jump to a lamp post.

Getting closer! Nax sent.

Putting on all the speed she could muster, Kila sent to Nax, *Meet me on top of the Cherry Bottom Inn.* Nax didn't have much sense of distance or direction, but she could unerringly find places she'd been before.

Kila's feet hit the tavern roof. The chasm of the Street of Sorrows opened before her. The lamp post stood five paces away. She did not slow.

Leaping into open air, she reached for the post. Her hands gripped the rough iron. Her momentum swung her in a full circle around it. At the end of the turn, she let go. She tucked into a ball, rotated, and extended her legs to land feet-first on the street.

Breath heaving, she ran straight across the street toward an alleyway.

Her vision shuddered in blurry flashes. She lost her balance and pitched forward. Instinct took over, sending her arms flailing and feet stumbling as she fought for balance.

The world shifted utterly. Her vision switched to a perspective outside of herself. Impossibly, she was looking down at the Street of Sorrows from a rooftop. She saw herself, tiny in the distance.

The catsight. She was seeing *through* Nax's eyes.

She fell. Her palms flamed as they scraped across the paving stones. Her stomach heaved as dizziness spun in her head. The vision didn't move, making her disorientation absolute.

Get up, Nax sent.

Kila felt the paving stones beneath her. The coppery taste of blood stained her tongue. In her vision, she was lying face-down on the street, arms stretched in front of her. She curled into a ball, tried not to cry out from the pain in her palms and knees.

She rolled onto her back. Still her vision was tied to Nax's. She retched.

They come. Get up, Nax urged.

Kila struggled to gather her breath. She had only experienced the catsight a couple of times before, and never for more than a few seconds. She tried to relax, to let her mind accept what she was seeing.

Get up, Kila!

She started to, but fell as Nax turned her eyes away from Kila. The vision swung wildly before her. Her mind fought to make sense of it. A figure in black slunk along rooftops, moving parallel to the Street of Sorrows. A shadow moving among the shadows. The figure's posture showed they were looking for a way down from the roof.

Kila! Get up!

I can't see. You're sending the catsight.

Oh.

Kila's vision snapped back to her own eyes. She rolled to her feet, gasping as her wounds flared from the movement. The skin on her palms and knees screamed as if slashed with a dull blade.

Hissing through her teeth, she glanced to the rooftops. The figure wasn't there.

Stifling her groans, Kila stumbled across the Street of Sorrows and into an alley. It was narrow and smelled of spoiled food and dumped chamber pots.

She knew one thing for sure. Her pursuer didn't know the roofway as well as she did, else they would have gotten to her while she was on the ground. They must have been following her for a while. Perhaps from the bell tower.

She must have drawn their attention coming down from the tower. But this wasn't a guard of the Watch following her. Not while wearing all black. Not without breastplate and a big sword on the hip.

Another thief, then. But why chase Kila?

Kila's hands were in no shape to climb. The knees of her pants were torn ragged. Blood trickled down her shins. She brushed the back of her hand against her lip. Blood there, too. She licked it away.

One of her front teeth wobbled a bit. If she lost a tooth because some Kil-licking thief had chased her off the roofway, she would hunt them down and return the favor. She didn't think much of her own appearance, but she was proud of her teeth.

She continued along the lane, working her way downhill toward the city wall and the Cheaps. If she could get into Cheapsgate, she'd be able to hide.

One problem with that. How would Nax get through? The cat didn't dare pass through the gate. One of the guards would scoop her up for the bounty. Failing that, he'd send flickbow bolts into her pelt.

The only other way out was through the sewers. But Nax couldn't lift the grate at bottom of Cherry Hill.

Nax? Can you still hear me?

Yes. The reply was thin in Kila's mind.

Get one of the boys to come to the grate and let you in.

No. They are coming to help you.

Are they inside the city?

Yes.

Instinct spun Kila. She caught a blur of black flying at her. Something silvery gleamed inside of it. She dropped to the pavement. A wisp of air ruffled her hair as someone passed over her.

Kila sprang up and backpedaled. The assailant turned with a sharp jerk and crouched in a fighting stance. The face was feminine, angular jaw, fine brows. Dark gaze.

Kila drew Cayne from its sheathe. Her shredded palm complained, but Kila kept her grip firm.

The woman was older than Kila. Considerably. An edge of gray hair peeked from her black hood. The woman's posture spoke of pure aggression. She was, quite simply, fury with black eyes.

"You will commme witt me," the woman said. Her voice was low, commanding, and strangely accented, every syllable stretched. Even Gristensiders, who spoke archly and precisely, didn't abuse consonants quite as fiercely.

"Why would I go with ya, dearie?" Kila said, instinctively falling into Cheaps-speak. "Ya tried to slice me with yer blade."

The woman's lips curled. A smile or a snarl, Kila couldn't tell. "Eef I meannnt to slize you, I would hyave." She flipped her blade, caught it in a reverse grip, and slipped it into a sheath tucked at the small of her back.

Kila did not relax her own fighting crouch. "So ya would kick me instead of slice me. That hardly makes us friends."

"No." The woman took one short step toward Kila. She dragged out her words, as if she were pronouncing the laws of Kil himself. "I chall be honestt witt you, Kila Sigh. I mmeann to beat you into submmmeession. You can nnnyot defffeat mme, evennn witt your styolen blate."

Kila didn't know what to object to first: the threat, the use of her full name, or the accusation that her blade was stolen. "Who told ya my name, old lady?"

This brought a smile to the woman's eyes. Kila had to admit, her face—what she could see of it—was quite beautiful.

Even though the lane lay in darkness, a glimmer caught in the woman's eyes. "You are well knyown to the Watchhh."

That was true, unfortunately. It struck Kila as odd that the Watch would employ a person like this. For one, they were mostly led by men. And two, they hated bounty hunters. And that's what this woman had to be.

"Come at me, then," Kila said. "I'll give ya a stab or two before ya settle me."

Nax's voice broke into Kila's mind. *We are coming. Hurry.*

The thrill of the zing washed over Kila like a bucket of cold water. The pain in her hands, knees, and lip reached a crescendo. And yet there was a distance to it. More pain, but more bearable. Odd.

The woman wore black shoes. Like slippers. Kila heard the soft scuff as the soles pressed onto the paving stones.

Kila's own heartbeat thundered in her ears. The rasp of her breath brought her attention to her uncontrolled panting.

She took control of her breath. Just because the woman threatened to beat her unconscious didn't mean she was capable of doing so.

Still . . . The woman moved with the confident fluidity of one well-practiced in the ways of violence. Kila's father had moved that way, too.

Kila waited for the attack, determined to make the woman pay with blood for every blow she received.

A flurry of black came at her. Kila thrust Cayne at it. Her body jerked forward, thrown by the assailant as easily as Kila could toss a rag doll. Kila's momentum thrust her into a brick wall. Her acute hearing warned her of approaching footsteps, then silence.

Kila rolled. Her attacker struck the wall where Kila had been a moment before.

Cayne flashed out, meeting nothing but air.

The woman was good. Kila preferred fighting men who were out too late, weakened by liquor and the late hour. They fought stupidly, and her speed always overmastered their strength.

Kila never sought to win such fights, but merely to escape—hopefully with a fat purse in her hands. She'd happily settle for escaping this one with her life.

The woman was gone. Kila scanned the lane.

The skin-prickling sensation of eyes upon her made Kila spin. She checked the rooftops. Nothing.

"What is yer name, old lady?" she called.

The answer came as a flurry of fists. One caught Kila in the gut, folding her over. The next slammed her side. A spear of agony ripped a cry from Kila's lips. Something in her abdomen convulsed.

A third blow knocked her chin to the side. Her body followed, spinning to the ground.

Arms twined around Kila's then levered her off her feet. The stone street pounded into her ribs and cheek. She found herself pinned and immobilized by her attacker's legs.

A face pressed close to Kila's, the breath hot and spicy. "Submmmmitt, *child*."

Kila still held Cayne despite the abrasions on her palms screaming for her to let go. But the blade had been her father's. The only thing of his she had left. She bent her wrist all around, seeking with the tip of the blade.

She scraped her own forearm, drawing a hairline of blood. Desperate, she jerked the blade around. It caught nothing. Her attacker had accounted even for the limited range of Kila's weapon.

Kila locked eyes with the hateful woman. The look Kila found there was vague and unfocused. The woman's lips parted, writhing as if she was fighting with herself.

The more Kila strained against the woman's hold, the more tightly she squeezed. The agony of Kila's wounds now gave way to new pain as her arms were pulled farther behind her back.

The woman twisted one of Kila's arms, sending shredding agony through Kila's shoulder. Still she held her attacker's gaze. Defiance was at the core of Kila's heart, and it always came out in times of great danger.

Something was off about the woman's eyes. As if she were no longer at home inside her skull. "Who are you?" Kila rasped.

The woman's eyes rolled up, exposing only white orbs. "Kila Sigh. I have been looking for you."

The accent was gone. The voice was smooth. "Submit to my servant. It would be a shame if she injured you irreparably. Drop your weapon, cease your resistance. Allow your hands to be bound. My servant will bring you to me."

Kila realized her attacker was not speaking for herself. Someone—or something—was speaking through her.

Skin flashing cold with fear, Kila thrust her face toward her attacker. Her teeth sank into the flesh around the woman's right eyebrow.

The effect was instant.

Kila's arm was jerked up farther. Something popped in her shoulder. The world went white. Kila's scream rose to the sky, startling a roosting pigeon into panicked flight from a nearby rooftop.

An answering cry rose, too. The furious mewl of a cat.

Nax!

Coming.

Thumping noises sounded from down the lane, of someone leaping from a rooftop to the paving stones.

A boy's voice: "Let her go, ya Kil-lickin' whoreson!"

The pressure on Kila's body released. Her head thunked onto the ground.

The fluttering sound of loose clothing receded into the noise of heavy breathing. Hands grasped Kila. Her injured shoulder flared again. She cried out.

"Sorry, love," said Fallo. "You don't look well."

"Never thought I'd like to look upon yer face," she said. "But it's most welcome."

Fallo was her age. He looked like a villain from a mummer's skit. His one continuous eyebrow hung over both eyes like a black caterpillar's pelt. A scraggle of whiskers sprouted from his chin and waved aimlessly in the air.

He helped her up. She had to support her injured arm to keep it from sending lances of fire through her shoulder.

Nax appeared and leapt to her good shoulder. Kila raised a hand to scratch the cat between her ears. *Thanks for bringin' the brigade, Naxie.*

Nax answered with a mewl and nudge of her snout against Kila's ear.

Henley ran toward them from up the lane. Red hair floofed from beneath the edges of his black knit cap. "She's gone. Disappeared."

"She prolly took the roofway," Kila said.

Coughing sounded from the other direction. Wen jogged into view, holding a rag to his mouth. He stopped and wheezed. "You're still living, sister?" His ornery cat, Oly, crept next to him, mushed face looking dour and disapproving, creamy fur bristling.

Wen never used the word "sister" unless he was angry or worried. Kila guessed he was a little of both right now. He'd told her not to come to Terriside alone.

"She's wounded," Fallo said.

"I can see that." Wen straightened and eyed Kila's injuries. "Finta Sahng is not too far. Can you walk?"

Henley took the lead, and Fallo fell back into position as the rear guard. An upwelling of warmth toward both boys brought an ache to Kila's throat. Not long ago, these scamps had been her enemies. But then they'd bonded to the cats and somehow that had made them family.

Kila checked the rooftops as they stumbled down the lane. She didn't spot any of the boys' cats. And that was as it should be. *Nax, you should go up top.*

She sensed the resistance through the bond. But cats possessed a strong sense of self-preservation, bond or no. Nax jumped down. Her slim gray form wisped into the shadows like a puff of smoke.

Soon Kila sensed the animal on the rooftops, pacing her as they continued downslope toward Finta's shop.

6

ATLEN MANURE

"Who was that back there?" Wen asked.

"We weren't exchangin' names. The way she talked, her tongue was fightin' with our language." Kila described the odd moment when the woman seemed to be overtaken with someone else's voice.

"I told you the Watch had a burr in their helmets over you, sister. Radiant Hiolly threw a tantrum at Captain LiTishke after you got caught on his property. You should have listened to me and stayed well out of Terriside."

"She wasn't of the Watch, *brother*."

"How do you know? That woman has skills the Watch do not. Perhaps they hired her to track you down."

"The Watch would stick a flickbow bolt into Her Enlightened Majesty's backside before dropping gold skillets into a bounty hunter's paws. That woman works for someone else."

"Who?"

"I don't have the first clue."

But that wasn't entirely true. She recalled the sedan chair, borne by a team of strong men. And Dunne Skyll with his paralyzing mercus wand, who'd told her the skeletal man inside the chair wanted her. He'd never said for what, but he'd been clear it wasn't good. She hadn't mentioned any of that to Wen.

If the woman worked for that horrid living corpse, Kila would have to lay low for a while.

"Maybe it has to do with the cats," Henley said.

Wen arched an eyebrow and nodded. "Word has gotten around. I won't deny it."

"Let's ask Finta," Kila said, wishing to drop the subject entirely.

They turned a corner, and Finta's small shop and home came into view. They ducked alongside to the rear entrance. The structure was old, but well-kept. Plank siding seamed snugly with pitch and painted fresh every few years.

There was no light in the upstairs window. It was well past dinner, but Kila hoped the old woman was still awake. Her shoulder throbbed, and her arm didn't work quite right.

Wen knocked. The door wasn't latched and swung open into darkness.

"She always locks it," Kila said, the zing returning

and magnifying her aches and pains even as it distanced them. "Always."

At this hour, Kila would expect a lit lantern or candle in Finta's home. But all was dark inside.

Wen guided Kila into the small, tidy kitchen. Light bloomed as he lit a fish-oil lantern. They both knew the kitchen well, having shared tea there with Finta many times.

Wen dropped the ash of the flashtaper he'd used into the small hearth. He held a hand over the coals there. "Warm. Not hot."

Henley returned from the front shop where Finta met with patients and sold her healing concoctions. He shook his head.

Stairs squeaked as Fallo climbed to the little bedroom over the shop. He returned to the kitchen moments later. "She isn't here. The bedclothes aren't rumpled."

"She must have forgotten to pull the door closed all the way when she stepped out," Henley said.

A row of cats marched in, Nax in the lead. Kila's cat wove between her shins. Lop, a floof of black fur on legs, went to Fallo. Huff, a short-haired orange tabby, went to Henley.

Kila's creamy white nemesis, Oly, butted his head into Wen's leg until the boy bent to pick him up.

Fallo and Henley didn't know Finta as well as Kila and Wen did. But they both knew the ancient woman hadn't had an absent-minded moment in all of her one hundred years.

Kila took a seat and rested her arms on the worn round table. The place smelled of Finta's minty tea and smoke from the flashtaper. And something else.

Do you smell anything unusual? she sent to the small gray.

Nax's nose wiggled. *No.*

Ask the others. A smell that doesn't belong here.

Why didn't you ask that to start with? There is atlen dung.

That was it. Kila smelled it distinctly now that Nax had identified it. Atlens were huge birds, cheaper to maintain than horses, and fleeter of foot. They pulled wagons and carriages. Their eggs were tasty, too.

"Boys," Kila said, "do you see any atlen manure on the floor?"

Henley and Fallo looked around their feet. Fallo's eyebrow lowered. "We've bathed three times. We can't possibly still stink of the atlen barn."

"I'm not accusing you of stinking. Nax smells the droppings here."

Wen squinted at her, then studied the floor. "Oly smells it, too."

Soon the boys were scanning the floor of the shop. Henley found the smudge, a line of white and black goo. "Like off somebody's boot," he said.

Kila stayed in the kitchen, trying to hold the arm of her injured shoulder still. Even without moving it, the shoulder throbbed. "Someone besides Finta was here. And now she's gone."

"Atlen droppings are common in the streets," Fallo said. "This doesn't mean much."

Wen cut off Kila's angry retort with a wave of his hand. She swallowed her first response. "My dear Fallo," she said, imitating his proper diction. "Finta Sahng does not leave the shop with so much as a speck of dirt on the floor."

Fallo didn't seem to catch her mocking imitation. Henley did, but had the wisdom to hide his grin. He was two years younger than Fallo, and the victim of frequent retaliatory shoulder punches.

"Maybe somebody broke in here after she left," Fallo said. "A thief."

"What did they take?" Kila asked.

The boys looked around, but it was impossible to say what was missing when they didn't know what Finta owned in the first place. Nothing looked disturbed. There were no empty spots on Finta's medicine shelves.

"There's another possibility," Wen said. The words tumbled out, as if he'd rather not give voice to them.

But Kila was already there. "Someone took her."

7

HARLOTS AND CRONES

S omeone else sought the girl.

The burst of mercus power in the city had flared in the Hargothe's awareness like a falling star. Brilliant and fleeting. It left a trail resonating on the mercusine. Someone had expended an enormous amount of power just now. He knew of few people capable of such a feat.

The trail told him all. It had originated from the Baths of Ori. So, the Voluptuary had felt the girl's awakening. Frustrating, but not surprising. No coincidence that Kila Sigh had sparked brightly upon the mercusine at the same time the other burst had flared. He'd even detected her spark spirit companion, the cat.

If the harlots captured the girl first, he'd lose his best chance to explore and exploit her. Intolerable.

The Hargothe rang his silver bell. Moments later

his elderly servant tiptoed in. Even so, the swish of his robes grated on the Hargothe's overly-sensitive ears.

"Yes, Seer Hargothe?"

"Send word to Highest Chilow. The Voluptuary knows of Kila Sigh. Ask him to redouble his efforts to secure her before the Way of the Harlot does."

"Yes." The man backed away, leaving the Hargothe to stew in anger and frustration. If Chilow failed in this simple task, perhaps it was time to replace him. The order of Donse Masters was a bloated bureaucracy, and it had elevated a moron to its highest seat.

Too long had the Hargothe slumbered. No more. It was time to take a more active role in the governance of the Abbey. The harlots and crones had to be put back into their places, their power focused toward the service of Til.

First the Hargothe would assert control here, and then—in due time—he would summon the Voluptuary to this room and accept her obeisance, too.

Feeding off the boy earlier had invigorated him enough to sit up. His mind felt clearer.

He wanted another.

8

NOT SO LUCKY

The passage back to Cheapsgate was pure torture. Climbing down to the sewers and navigating the tunnels to the huge outlet that dumped water into Sourwater Inlet took three times longer than usual.

But it was that or go through the Cheaps. With the cats along, that was out of the question.

And given Kila's run-in with the black-clad woman earlier—and Finta's odd disappearance—Wen had refused to let Kila risk passing through the Cheaps by herself. The Watch was after her and, bruised or no, they would recognize her in an instant.

By the time they got to Critt Sanglo's tavern along the docks near their home, Kila had gone pasty and cold from pain. Wen didn't look much better. A coughing fit had reddened his kerchief. Fallo half-carried Kila into the tavern.

Seeing them, the huge proprietor jerked his head toward the back room.

Critt Sanglo's was nothing like a Terriside establishment. For one, it was illegal. For two, it was inside the upside-down hull of an old ship. The ribs of the keel arched overhead, forming a long echoey room thirty paces long.

A door in the back led to an addition made from the usual Cheapsgate building materials. Namely, whatever junk Sanglo had been able to find. This back apartment was Critt's home. A bed hunkered along one wall, a battered brass lamp on a wooden crate next to it. Shelves displayed the weird trophies of his sailing days: odd skulls, ornate vases, a few books with lurid paintings of naked women, and pieces of whalebone etched with scenes of sailor life.

He followed the troupe of thieves into his room. He eyed Kila. "Ya look like Kil chewed on ya afore spittin' ya to the wind."

"Thankee, Critt," Kila said, working up a rueful smile.

The man's barrel-like torso was padded with fat, but beneath that lay thick layers of muscle. His forearms looked like ham hocks. His hair was tied back in a sailor's queue and tarred. Nobody said Critt was handsome. But even with several teeth absent from his grin, he exuded a unique charm. He had been Father's friend, and thought of Wen and Kila as nephew and niece.

"She was attacked," Wen said, helping Fallo ease Kila onto Critt's bed.

The man spat a glob of greenish chew at a spittoon across the room. "Attacked? Naw. You was *beaten*, lassie."

Kila laughed humorlessly. "Was wonderin' if you'd shove my shoulder into shape."

"Ya came to me for doctorin'? Me mother would be proud to hear it, weren't she long dead and sunk in the Sourwater."

"Finta Sahng wasn't home," Wen said. He glanced at the boys to keep them from volunteering any more than that.

Kila didn't know why Wen was bothering to keep Finta's disappearance secret. But that was just how he was. Cautious.

"We know what happens in yer 'stablishment, Critt," Kila said, wincing as he probed her shoulder with sausage-thick fingers. "Ya bind more broken legs than an army sawbones after battle."

Critt Sanglo said nothing. Didn't need to. A tavern-keep had to know the basics of wound-tending. Fights were a daily occurrence.

"I once met a man wi' no right arm," Critt said. He took hold of Kila's elbow and wrist, pulling her forearm away from her belly. She gasped, but managed to stifle a cry. Henley was making great effort not to watch, his face slightly green. "We called him Lefty, o' course."

Kila wished for Nax's comforting presence but wasn't about to bring a cat into a place like this. Critt might be friendly, but he wouldn't think twice about taking a cat straight to the Abbey for Til's bounty.

Critt continued his story. "Lefty served as a able seaman in Her Enlightened's Navy. I asked him, 'Mate, how'd ye come to lose yer starboard yard?' And do you know what he said?"

Critt made her shrug her shoulder up then pinned her elbow to her side. The pressure built in her shoulder as he rotated her arm outward. Kila didn't know why he was doing what he was doing, but she wished he'd just get on with it.

Nobody answered, so Critt continued, "The old sailor said, 'Thick 'o battle, Critt lad. I were on the fo'c'scle, about to clamber the bowsprit t' strike the spanker when a Yinman's hardblast shot found the crook o' me elbow. The ball ripp'd muh lower arm right off. Had the upper stub a'danglin' in th' breeze and gushin' blood like a bilge pump.'"

Critt waggled Kila's arm until she yelped. He smiled at her. "So I asked him, 'but there be no stub now? What happen to it?'"

Critt pulled Kila's forearm away from her, elbow still pinned to her side. The pain drew a curse from Kila's throat. Critt nodded appreciatively, then said, "Ol' Lefty says to me, he says, 'Critt, I ne'er gave no ship to the talents of the sawbones. Lost more'n one mate t' their ministrations. So I claps a line to m'stub and loops it round a capstan. I shout for me mates to heave it 'round while I brace m'self against the main mast. Three turns and *pop!'"*

With a firm yank and push, Critt seated Kila's shoulder. It clunked into place.

Henley sucked air through his teeth as if he'd suffered the re-socketing of his own arm.

Relief pulled a sigh out of Kila.

Fallo laughed at Critt's story. "What a lie. You can't pull your arm off with a rope."

Critt didn't laugh. "A sailor what knows his blocks and tackle, why he can move near anythin', lad."

Fallo continued laughing and waved the comment away.

"Thankee, Critt Sanglo," Kila said. "I don't have more'n a copper plug to offer ya."

"Keep it, girlie. I'll take a favor." He winked. "When I have need of your partic'lar sneak skills."

They filed out of Critt's room and into the tavern. A few more patrons had wandered in. Kila tugged on Critt's arm. "Have ya ever seen a woman here all in black? Fighter way of walkin'?"

"Everyone comes here has a fighter way of walkin'."

"Not a brawler," Kila said. "Trained. Tall as me, older. Touch o' gray in her hair. Handsome face. Fancy with a blade. Tongue that wrestles with words and slams 'em out."

Critt's eyes stayed vague and disinterested until that last bit. "An accent, ya say?"

Kila imitated it. "Commme witt me or I chall beatt you to deatt."

Recognition flared in Critt's eyes. "Alnassi, sounds like. Where did ya see such a woman?"

"Roofways o' Terriside. She did all this bruisin' to me."

Critt's nostrils quirked. "A dire enemy you've made, lass."

"Would the Watch pass a gold skillet bounty to one of these . . . Alnassi?"

"No. Ya canna hire Alnassi. They does what they does—and kills who they kills—for their own reasons. Gold ne'er held much charm for 'em."

Kila didn't want to say more. If the Alnassi woman was after her, she might come to Cheapsgate and start asking questions here. Besides, how could she tell Critt the woman had been overtaken by some spirit and suddenly spoke without the accent?

With a final nod of thanks to Critt Sanglo, she and the boys climbed to the rooftops and headed back toward their den in the Warren. Fallo and Henley ranged ahead. The cats rejoined Kila and Wen, holding close to their people. Kila's run-in had ruffled them all.

You will rest now, Nax sent to Kila. It wasn't a question.

Yes.

She had to go slowly anyway. Wen had a coughing

fit, which doubled him over. She rubbed his back and glared at a few passersby who came too close.

Gasping, brow glistening with sweat, Wen started moving again. He held his arms close to his chest, as if chilled. "I don't think any of this is a coincidence. You attacked. Finta missing."

Kila hadn't connected the two events. But Wen had a fair point. It was no secret that Finta had been making medicines for Wen.

"Ya think the Alnassi woman dragged her off? Given the timin', she would have to have done it before attackin' me."

"We're not at Critt Sanglo's anymore, so stop it with the Cheaps talk," Wen said. He never liked her to use the patois of the slums. "As for Finta? Maybe the Alnassi woman took her. Maybe she was questioning Finta about you. And about Nax."

Without a word sent either way Nax leapt into Kila's arms, which were waiting to receive her. The slim gray was light, almost birdlike, in her arms, fur soft and comforting under her fingers.

Wen was right. Many people knew about the cats now. As stealthy as they tried to be, it was impossible to traverse the city without being spotted occasionally. And Finta knew all about the cats.

"But maybe it wasn't the same woman who attacked you," Wen said, brows furrowed as his mind churned over the question.

"If it wasn't the Alnassi woman, then who?"

"No reason to think that woman was working alone."

The thought chilled Kila. "What should we do, brother?"

Wen jerked around to look at her. She realized she'd called him brother, exposing how much the attack and Finta's disappearance had rattled her.

"Not sure we can do much for poor old Finta," he said as they descended toward the front entrance of the Warren. The cats slipped away into shadows. They had their own ways into the sprawling slum, ways that would keep them hidden from greedy-hearted folk.

A thug the size of a fishing boat stood next to the sliding door to the Warren. His bludgeon leaned against the wall in a not-so-subtle warning to troublemakers.

"Good evenin', Jocko," Kila said as they passed into the noisome Warren. The smells of cooking rat meat made her stomach growl.

Jocko tilted his head ever so slightly. "Parlo Odok is wantin' t' talk ter both o' ya."

Kila didn't want to talk to the Warren's landlord. She wanted to lie down and sleep for a couple years. She was about to tell Jocko how the Warren's landlord could talk to a certain part of his own arse when Wen touched her arm. He gave her a stern look.

She clamped her teeth together and followed her brother. Parlo Odok's office was also his own den. It was much larger than the other compartments built into the old warehouse.

The Warren sat along an abandoned stretch of the old docks. Dead fish smells from Sourwater Bay were especially strong here. Not that Odok would notice. He wore a sheen of filth on his skin like underclothing.

The man was in his fourth ten-year, Kila thought. Bald as her naked left buttock, narrow shoulders draped with a disgusting woolen shirt, and trousers made out of holes. Considering how much rent he pulled in, he lived like a destitute trezz fiend.

The reason for all this, Kila knew, was because Parlo Odok was as cheap as he was greedy.

He eyed Wen and Kila with suspicion. His den had no furniture and he never burned a lantern if he could avoid it, instead relying on light coming from the den across the hall. There wasn't much illumination, so he was just a dark shape in the gloom.

"I'm happy t' see ya both alive," Parlo Odok said. "Summun was askin' round for ya. A woman. She didna look exceptional frinnly to me, no she didna."

Kila's skin thrilled. "All in black, handsome face, a bit o' the gray in her hair?"

"Sounds like me own lusty dreams, th' way ya describes her. But no, that weren't the one I spoke to. This maid were young as yer own self. And nice 'n well-fed." He made squishing motions with his fingers and grinned enough to show his tooth. "She offer'd me five gold skillets fer yer where'bouts."

Wen shoved Kila toward the door. "Run!"

Kila didn't have a chance to consider the command. Jocko had his arms around her, lifting her from the floor. She struggled, but the huge man pinned her arms. Her flailing feet had no more effect on his shins than kicking a boulder.

Odok stood, blade flashing in his filthy hand. "Relax yerself. No sense gettin' yer hide sliced open. Fightin' will come ta nothin' but grief for ya."

Kila tried her biting trick, but her teeth couldn't do more than dent Jocko's leather sleeve. It tasted like a sewer rat's underbelly. She spat in disgust.

Wen started coughing. The convulsions were so violent he was forced to one knee. Odok patted Wen's shoulder as he passed him and approached Kila.

Naxie, I'm gonna be late back to the den.

Why?

Odok sold me out to . . . somebody.

I'm coming.

To Jocko the slumlord said, "Keep 'er held tight."

Jocko never said anything he didn't have to. He started walking, Kila squeezed to his chest like a keg of ale. Odok followed, stopping to shut the door to his own den. He fumbled with a lock. Kila heard a sharp click.

"Ya sure ya want to leave Wen alone in yer den, Odok?" Kila said.

"I keep nothin' o' value in there."

"Where *do* ya keep yer treasure?"

Jocko hefted Kila into one arm while he shoved the Warren's front door aside. He plucked up his bludgeon and gave Kila's head a gentle tap with it to let her know what to expect if she struggled.

She relaxed as much as she could. The zing was rising, though she couldn't see that it would help much.

Odok started to lead the way, taking a crude stairway of crates to the roofs of Cheapsgate. "I'll tell ya where I keep muh gold when we meet down in Kil's great tavern, lass. The drinks'll be on Til's tab then."

Jocko laughed, making his chest and belly jump. His breath was redolent of smoked fish and beer.

"I hope ya choke on yer drink, Odok," Kila said through gritted teeth. "Truly, I do. But if I ever get free o' this lout, I'll be chokin' you with my own hands."

"Get in line, lass."

Odok always had to have the last word. Kila didn't care. If keeping her mouth shut kept his shut, that was just fine with her.

"I can walk upon my own feet," she said to Jocko.

He grunted skeptically and tightened his hold on her.

She had to admit it was a good decision on his part. If he'd set her down, she'd be gone faster than an atlen with its tail feathers on fire.

She felt Nax approaching. *Stay back,* she warned. *The boys are coming.*

Jocko will kill them.

Like the rest of Starside, Cheapsgate went uphill. The Warren, being on the old docks, stood at the lowest point. The rest of the slum climbed toward the city wall.

There were no streets in Cheapsgate, just a maze of winding alleys and a thousand dead ends. Kila knew most of them. If you wanted to get where you were going, you walked the roofs.

The ramshackle buildings followed no plan. Their roofs were tarred, shingled, or sometimes bare planks. None of the material was new; most of it was salvaged from ships or shipping crates.

The sun was long dead and the moon not risen. The roofways were dark as Kil's heart. There were a few people about, drunkards and villains mostly. Nax was close, but Kila couldn't see the little gray.

Stay out of sight.

The cat didn't respond.

Cheapsgate wasn't like Terriside, where people feared mere robbery. Here, murder might claim you for no other reason than a man didn't like the looks of you.

Nobody was going to attack Parlo Odok, though. Not with Jocko along. She sent to Nax, *Tell Fallo and Henley not to do anything stupid. They can't take Jocko—*

She's coming!

Who?

Her!

A black shadow tumbled toward them, somersaulting in a flurry of ruffling fabric. The acrobatics startled the two men, freezing them in a momentary stupor of amazement. Then the attacker was upon them.

Jocko shifted Kila to one arm and clamped her to his body with the strength of an iron band. He swung his bludgeon in a huge arc. It cut empty air.

Explosive grunts came through Jocko's nose as blows landed on his body. Then Parlo Odok cried out and fell backward off the rooftop.

Jocko whirled and swung wildly.

One second the Alnassi stood before him, arms raised and fingers pressed together to make blades of her hands, and the next she was sliding beneath his blow and striking two, three, four punches and kicks in quick succession.

Jocko wobbled and cursed.

"Drop her, Yock-oh," the woman said. No hint of breathlessness in her voice. She might have been out for an evening stroll. "I weery of thees borink commbat."

The huge man swore and threw his club. The tactic surprised the Alnassi woman, and she arched backward. The massive club passed just over her nose, then clunked onto the rooftop and tumbled into an alley.

The woman shot into the air, leg swinging. Kila

tried to turn her head away. It wasn't necessary. The flying kick took Jocko in the jaw.

The world spun as Jocko twirled like a dancer. He fell onto his back, cushioning Kila's fall. His arm went limp.

She rolled off him and sprang to her feet. She did not look for the black-clad woman but instead ran away, hoping to drop to the alley level. Hands caught her shoulder, a foot pressed into the crook of her knee. She fell back.

Air rushed from her lungs as she struck the rooftop.

The familiar, beautiful face loomed over her. "Thees time I theenk you nnot so lucky."

A sharp stab flared on Kila's neck, just like one of Nax's claws sinking into her skin.

Her head felt very heavy. Her mind sodden. Thoughts struggled to form and the night sky retreated.

Nax? she sent.

She did not hear the cat's response. If there was any at all.

9

TOUCHED BY TIL

Henley Mast huddled in the Warren den, his cat Huff on his lap. His best friend Fallo lay on the floor across from him, Lop already asleep on his belly.

The run-in with the Alnassi fighter kept repeating in Henley's mind. "That woman moved faster than any fighter I've ever seen," he said. "I used to go to the pits with my father. He sponsored a man from the Watch one season. They moved around in circles and pummeled each other in the face. But this woman would have made short work of any of them."

"Alnassi are a strange people," Fallo said. "Didn't your ships trade with them?"

"Their harbor at Fassin-Syk was open to us, but trezz isn't popular there. They prefer wine from their own vineyards. I went ashore once—that was before my brother got murdered by one of the Keels.

Anyway, I didn't see anyone fighting like that woman."

"There's all sorts of people in every little place."

"As true as that?"

"As true as that."

The scrap of rug that covered the door pushed in. Wen fell into the den after it.

Huff and Lop leapt to their feet at the same moment.

Kila is in trouble, Huff sent.

"What happened?" Fallo said to Wen, helping him up.

Wen coughed and spit out a tangle of phlegm and blood. Every time he tried to speak, another bout of coughing hit him.

Huff, Henley sent, *ask Oly what's happened.*

Oly doesn't know. Nax says people took Kila.

Lop must have told Fallo the same, for he squatted next to Wen, who now lay on his pallet, breath wheezing in and out. "Who took Kila?"

Huff's voice returned to Henley's mind. *Wen told Oly the name Parlo Odok. And Jocko.*

The landlord and his strongman. They must have been paid off by the Alnassi woman. Or whoever she worked for.

Ask Nax where Kila is now, Henley sent to Huff.

Nax is too far away. She's running after . . . the woman.

A flash of image appeared in Henley's thoughts. The Alnassi fighter, Kila over her shoulder.

Wen convulsed and started to choke. Spittle bubbled at the corners of his mouth, tinged red. Fallo pushed the boy onto his side and patted his back. With a jerk, Wen spat out another glob. He inhaled deeply and wiped tears from his eyes.

"I need my medicine." He clutched his chest. "It feels like a weight is pressing on me."

Henley and Fallo exchanged a long glance. They didn't need to talk to know what each was thinking. They had to find Finta Sahng for the medicine, but they couldn't just let Kila get dragged away.

"I'll go after Kila," Henley said.

"We can't leave Wen here alone."

"I can walk," Wen said. "Take me back to Critt Sanglo's."

BY THE TIME Henley and Fallo left the tavern, the sun was high and bright. Their cats joined them in the sewer passage that led beneath the city wall. They came out in Starside, at the grate below Cherry Bottom hill.

"Huff says Nax is that way," Henley said, pointing west. "He can't talk to her, so I guess she's way up near the Abbey or beyond."

"At least you know that much. I'm going back to Finta's. I'll see if I can find more of Wen's medicine.

And maybe we overlooked something there that will lead to Kila or the old woman."

Henley hadn't been out on his own in the city since joining up with Fallo. It hadn't been that long ago, but so much had happened since. They'd met Kila, they'd found their cats. And now this. But he'd changed from the spoiled son of a rich merchant to a somewhat streetwise thief. "See you back at the Warren."

Fallo's eyebrow rose and he made a mocking bow. "I'll beat you there."

They climbed to the roofs and went their separate ways. Henley didn't have half of Kila's speed or a tenth of her fearlessness when it came to leaping over alleyways. It wasn't until he dropped to the street to pass through Dunne Medow Plaza that Huff finally spoke to Nax.

She says Kila is in a place.

What place?

A vision appeared in Henley's mind. A bell tower next to a domed building. The Baths of Ori. That was odd. He'd assumed the Watch was behind her kidnapping.

Huff continued along rooftops and through alleys, taking care to avoid being seen, while Henley strode through vast plaza. Sculptures in the huge central fountain depicted the bare-breasted Aslana kissing Kil, while her prim-faced sister Ori tried to pull her away. Not a soul was in the plaza with him. That was odd.

The hair on his neck prickled at the sound of footsteps behind him. Henley glanced back. A hooded man in the robes of a Donse Master followed him.

Henley didn't fit in here, dressed as he was in Cheapsgate rags. He'd allowed his ginger hair to grow back recently, choosing to conceal it beneath a knit cap. But a sudden chill warned him the Donse Master might have recognized him. The Keels still wanted him dead, and few Donse Masters would hesitate turning Henley over to them.

He continued toward the Trialti Arch which exited the plaza into Gristenside. The Baths were that way anyway. Maybe his worry was all in his mind. Why wouldn't a Donse Master be here? The Abbey's entrance was just beyond the fountain.

He increased his pace. Once he got to the shadows of the Arch, he'd put on more speed and get out of sight before the Donse Master got through.

Three more Donse Masters stepped from the arch, blocking his way. The center one held up his hands. "Hold, lad. You need not fear us."

Henley backed away. The trailing Donse Master lowered his hood, exposing a flow of gray hair and a short white beard. Henley didn't recognize him.

"I am Dunne Qirl, Seeker of the Way of Til," he said. "You may not feel it yet, but you are on the verge of awakening to the mercus."

Every word the man said went into Henley's head easily, but none of it made the slightest sense. He didn't have any mercus powers. No one in his family had ever possessed the slightest spark.

"I have urgent business in Gristenside. I'll stop by the Abbey when I'm done."

"I cannot allow it. You have been touched by Til. Now you must serve him." Dunne Qirl removed a short rod from his belt. It looked like the haft of a gardener's hand spade. The man held it forth. "I ask you to come with me. If you refuse, I will force you. You will not like it."

Henley ran straight at the man. The plaza was wide and Henley thought he could outrun anyone dressed in Donse Master's robes.

His second step came up short as his leg froze in place. He tumbled forward, arms suddenly locked and unable to extend to break his fall. His chin struck the flagstones and his brain erupted in red light.

10

SHE'S SHY

Fallo and Lop studied the inside of Finta Sahng's little shop. The smear of atlen dung was still there. But neither saw anything to suggest where the woman had gone. And there were no prepared tinctures anything like what Wen needed.

To help Wen, he had to find Finta. The only thing to do now was ask around. He went to the neighboring home, a moderately well-kept shack. A woman answered his knock by opening her door an inch. Her spotty face was lit by a slash of sunlight. The rest of her house was dark, curtains drawn. "Go away now. Get!" she said.

"I'm looking for Finta Sahng."

"She's gone. Tooken off."

"Who, uh, tookened her?"

The door shut in his face, followed by the sound of a bar latch scraping into its braces.

Fallo shouted through the door, "I need her medicine for my friend."

Nothing.

"I'm going to stay out here until you tell me."

Still no reply. A door on the other side of Finta's shop opened. A sturdy man peered out, face like a fist. The sign above his door read, LEET'S LEATHERNS & FOOTWARE.

"Ahoy, Master Leet," Fallo called. "Did you see where Finta Sahng was dragged off to?"

The man pulled into his shop and closed the door. Fallo kept talking as if the man were still there looking at him. "Don't tell anyone I'm calling on this woman here. She's shy. Yes, I know it's early, but a man has his needs. Oh, I didn't think so either, but you should see her when—"

The door opened wide and an iron skillet swiped through the air. Fallo ducked in time. His hand shot up to catch her wrist and halt a blow coming on the backswing. "I truly am sorry to inconvenience you, Miss . . ."

"Missus! And you get outta cheer!"

"Finta Sahng was kidnapped. What did you see?"

The woman fixed him with angry blue eyes. She had to be deep into her third ten-year, but Fallo found her plump figure rather comely. He flashed a smile.

"Yer as ugly as a boil on me brother's backside," she said.

"Thank you. Now, where is Finta?"

The woman cackled and lowered her skillet. "Thinnies. I saw 'em take her out. She weren't dragged, tho. She went willing enough."

Fallo gave her a mocking bow. "That wasn't too painful, was it?"

"Easier th'n lookin' atcha."

"You are too kind." Fallo pushed the door closed in her face.

Thinnies. This wasn't going to be easy. In fact, it was likely to get him killed.

Lop, we need to find a sewer grate close by. Lop? Wake up!

The cat roused herself. She passed sleepy irritation to Fallo, along with a feeling of fur rubbed the wrong direction.

The search didn't take long. Fallo merely followed a trickle of rain runoff down an alley. It dripped into a huge iron grate. He stooped and lifted. Surprisingly, the grate was hinged on one side. He spotted a counterweight dropping away into the gloom below. It wasn't uncommon for thinnies to make hatches from grates to make climbing to the street easier.

A rusty ladder led down. He'd been in the sewers once before, for a very brief time. Not pleasant. But he'd seen worse. At least there weren't likely to be ghosts down there.

Hop on, Lop.

The furry black cat didn't hop so much as present

herself to be lifted. She settled on Fallo's shoulder, digging claws into his shirt for better purchase.

"You know, Lop, maybe life in the atlen barn wasn't so bad."

Eggs!

And into darkness they descended.

11

THE MEANING OF THE WORD

Swirls of light.

Bright. Then night. A bite.

Flying above the Divide. A dragon swoops and dives. The bells of Starside. Father died. Wen coughs and tries to survive. He dies. Kila tries to climb, high, high, high. Nax rides.

A raven flies.

It cries: "Kila Sigh! Kila Sigh! Why won't you die? Why, Kila Sigh? Why? Why? Why?"

"Kila Sigh, wake up."

A warm hand rested Kila's forehead. Another gripped her arm, fingers pressed to the inside of her wrist.

"Your heartbeat is strong, child. The *filla* fever recedes." The voice was female, but low. It carried the resonance of age.

Though it took all her will, Kila managed to open

her eyes. Her mind was heavy with sleep. She remembered the battle on the Cheapsgate roofway. The Alnassi woman taking her down. No fear bubbled up in her body. Weariness wouldn't make room for it.

A woman with white hair sat next to Kila. A fire burned softly in a hearth across the room. Kila didn't recognize the place. Brickwork. Tidy. No furnishings except the cot she lay on and the stool the woman occupied.

The woman. High cheekbones, regal brow. Lines around the eyes and mouth, but not deep. She was striking.

"I'm Renna, Sensual of Ori." She smiled, showing wide, strong teeth. Something glimmered in her mouth. A piercing of gold on her tongue. "You are Kila Sigh."

"So you're the one who sent the Alnassi woman to fetch me?"

"No. But the one who sought you will be here soon. My task is to assist you when you need to be sick."

As if the words summoned the feeling, Kila's stomach rebelled. Her limbs failed to respond as she fought to roll onto her side. Renna helped Kila turn. A basin lay on the floor next to the cot, ready for Kila. "Relax," the woman crooned. "Let your body do what it needs to do."

Kila's body was going to do what it needed to do whether she relaxed or not. Her abdomen convulsed and a thin stream of black, bilious liquid came up. It splattered into the porcelain basin. The smell of sickup made Kila gag more.

"Good," Renna said. "That should do it."

The gentle woman fitted a cover on the basin and shoved it aside with her toe. Kila lay back and closed her eyes.

"The *filla* dose you received was small. The sickness will pass soon." Renna pushed Kila's chin, forcing her to turn her head to the side. With a light touch, the woman prodded Kila's neck. The spot where the Alnassi woman had stabbed Kila flared.

Renna dabbed a finger in a small jar, then swiped a cool poultice on Kila's wound. "The Alnassi are masters of the use of herbs for healing—and killing. Your heart was stilled for an hour or more, but *filla* preserves that which it poisons. To a point. A hair's weight separates a sleep dose from a death dose of *filla angocease*. Pol smiled upon you that Yiqa is so skilled, or you'd now be in the sleep eternal."

"Pol be damned," Kila said. "A better fortune to not be dosed at all."

Renna forced a tight smile as she turned Kila's face toward hers. "The wound is slight. Already it has closed. I noticed you had many more scrapes. You took a fall?" Renna pressed a hand ever so softly onto Kila's palm.

Kila recalled the scrapes she'd gotten falling on the Street of Sorrows. She looked at her other hand, not wanting to lose Renna's comforting touch. The scrapes were red, but healed over. She tried to lift her knees and look at them, but they were covered with a blanket.

And nothing else.

Awareness of her nakedness beneath the covers snapped her mind alert. "Where am I?"

"Safe. The Baths of Ori are a haven. Be at ease."

The Baths.

That told Kila she was in Gristenside, west of Dunne Medow Plaza. In fact, she had recently been near this very spot when she'd climbed the bell tower.

Nax? she sent. *Can you hear me?*

No response. She sensed the cat, far off to her right, but out of range of their silent communication. "A haven you call this, Sens Renna? I was attacked and dragged here by my hair."

"I assure you, you were carried most gently."

Kila started to object, but a new presence filled the small room. A waft of spicy air hit Kila's nose. Apples and something else she couldn't identify.

"Our feral kitten is finally home, I see." The voice chilled Kila. It was the same voice that had possessed the Alnassi woman during Kila's first encounter with her.

Sens Renna stood and kissed the new woman's cheek. "I'll wait outside."

Kila's new visitor was shorter than Renna. Stout and hardy. Her hair was a mix of gray and black, wiry, and pulled away from her blunt face. A sparkling hair-piece held the woman's hair back. Her robes were fine, and dark. Blue. Maybe purple. That meant they were expensive. "Don't get up, child."

Kila heard a note of sarcasm in the woman's words.

"Nice to fin'lly meet ya face ta face," Kila said. Since she couldn't stand up, using the Cheaps-speak was the best she could do to express her defiance. "Better than seein' yer Alnassi woman's eyes a'rollin' in their sockets."

"You are speaking to the Voluptuary of Ori, child. Respect won't kill you."

That explained Sens Renna's deference. The Voluptuary was the highest Sensual of the Way of Ori. Equivalent in rank—if not power—to the Highest of Til.

Kila didn't believe in Ori. The whole New Pantheon was a crock of atlen droppings as far as she was concerned. She thought better of saying this, considering who she was speaking to.

The Voluptuary plopped herself onto the stool and pressed her hand to Kila's forehead. She grabbed Kila's wrist and felt for her heartbeat.

"Sens Renna already did this routine," Kila said. "Mind tellin' me why ya sent that Alnassi to poison me?"

"I think you know."

"I don't have a sailor's clue in the desert."

The Voluptuary folded her hands in her lap and leveled an inquisitive stare at Kila. "You are a bit old for the mercus to be developing. But developing it is. Perhaps it's the cat. The Donse Masters think it is, I assure you."

Kila turned her face away.

"Oh, I know about your little gray friend, Kila Sigh. Your stunt atop my bell tower was fortuitous. I felt you up there. Pol's luck was with you. Had you done that close to Dunne Medow Cathedral, you would be at the mercy of a Donse Master even now. Or worse. Surely the Hargothe yearns for you."

Kila turned her face back. Her mouth went dry and shivers of fear snaked up her limbs. She saw again the sedan chair, the curtains concealing its horrid occupant. She saw how the men carrying it strode in short, slow steps. Her scalp squirmed as she remembered the feeling of that weird gaze. "The watcher . . ."

The Voluptuary hummed, then spoke. "Yes. You've felt his eyes upon you." She laughed softly. "I mean that figuratively, of course. The Hargothe surely doesn't *have* eyes. His ears are waxed to deafen him, and his skin is coated with numbing oils. He may even have burned out his sense of smell by sniffing the dried urine of rats." Her voice lilted over these horrors, as if telling an amusing anecdote over tea. "It depends how sensitive this one is."

The woman sensed Kila's confusion. Had probably

said all those things *intending* to confuse her, put her off balance.

Nax?

No answer.

The Voluptuary stroked Kila's brow. "Seers like him are highly attuned to the mercus. You know how it feels when it comes over you. Every smell and sound is sharp and distinct. Imagine that multiplied again and again. For some it is too much to bear, so Seers deaden their senses. This allows them to focus all their attention on the subtle world of mercus. That is how they detect people such as you."

"Am I s'posed to thank ya for havin' your woman poison me?"

"I expect someday you will. But I'm no fool. I can see things from your point of view. To protect you, I told Yiqa to do what she must."

Yiqa. *Yeekha*. So that's who Kila was going to have to kill. The Alnassi was tough. It wouldn't be easy. Kila set that aside. She was in no shape to stand up, much less face down a fearsome fighter like Yiqa.

But that reminded her . . . "Parlo Odok said a plump girl was askin' round for me in the Warren. Offered him five gold skillets for me. Odok and Jocko were takin' me somewheres to collect it when Yiqa came flippin' in from the dark."

The Voluptuary waved a small hand. "Parlo Odok would sell his feet to keep from having to buy shoes."

It seemed the Voluptuary knew what she was

talking about. "So yer saying that Alnassi bitc—*woman*—rescued me?"

"The woman Parlo Odok spoke of was not my agent. Perhaps she answers to the Highest, Dunne Chilow. The Way of Til does not want young talent like you in the hands of the Sensuals of Ori.

"An old healer I know went missin', too," Kila said. "Did yer mercenary take her, or did this other one?"

"Old healer? Who?"

"An ancient just inside the old wall. Finta Sahng."

The Voluptuary's face went stony. She stood and hugged her elbows. Her robes were not as thick as Kila had thought. They were layer upon layer of sheer fabric, each a different color. They fluttered purple and bluish as the woman paced the room.

"Finta is my sister. She was the eldest," the Voluptuary said. "She was a Sensual once, before she abandoned the order for her Alnassi man." She shrugged. "He's dead now. Finta learned much in her years among the Alnassi. Their command of plants for healing is unmatched. She can guard herself quite capably, I assure you. She probably went out of the city to gather ingredients for her tinctures."

Kila absorbed this strange information. It certainly explained Finta's knowledge. But Kila's gut insisted that something was amiss. She dropped the Cheapsspeak. "There was a smudge of atlen dropping on Finta's floor."

The Voluptuary stopped her pacing. "And she was absent from her shop?"

"We searched every room. The rear door wasn't locked when we got there."

"That is not like Finta." The Voluptuary's nostrils flared. "When were you there?"

"Earlier tonight. An hour after sunset."

A hard look came over the Voluptuary's face. "Someone must have been in dire need of her help. Perhaps a neighbor endured a difficult birth. Perhaps a child had a deathly fever. You need not concern yourself with Finta." The woman went to the door. "I'll speak with you when you've recovered. Sens Renna will attend you until then."

The Voluptuary departed and Sens Renna returned, calm and still. Her steps were fluid and she seemed to be in a sort of distant mindset. The world could shatter and Renna would sit back and notice it as the mere due course of things.

"You'll be hungry soon," she said. "Food is coming. And clothes. You have much to do."

"That's true enough," Kila said. "I want to get back to my brother."

"That is not what lies ahead for you."

"What is ahead for me?"

Renna smiled. "Your training, of course. I hear that Ori has made you flush with the Sensual mercus."

"I wouldn't know about sensual anything," Kila said uncomfortably. She'd heard startling rumors about what went on in this place. Renna was pretty and all, but Kila wasn't going to partake of some wild orgy with her. Boys were her flavor, though she hadn't yet met one who sparked much fire in her.

Renna stroked Kila's forehead. "You misunderstand the meaning of the word 'Sensual'. But you will learn. For now, relax. Enjoy good food. Rest. You will need it."

Kila found that she did need it. After her *filla* sleep, she should be jumping up and ready to run the roofway. But the mere thought of standing made her body want to curl up.

Only the smell of fresh bread and hearty soup got her to sit up. The food arrived on a simple wooden tray, carried by a girl no older than Kila.

The girl smiled and set the tray on Kila's lap. Before Kila could muster a thank you, the girl was gone. Renna had moved her stool to the far corner of the room. She sat there, eyes half closed and a small smile fixed on her face.

Kila ate. The food was good and her body seemed to draw strength from every bite. But once she had dabbed up every crumb of bread and scraped the wooden bowl clean of soup, a heaviness swarmed into her mind.

Content, and yet keenly aware she should be trying to escape, she curled into her blankets and closed her eyes. She reached out for Nax. The small gray's presence hovered far away, vague and tiny.

12

THE SENSUAL MERCUS

W hen gentle hands shook Kila awake, she sensed that an entire night had passed. Her mind felt clear.

"It begins," Sens Renna said.

"What does?"

"Your training."

Kila sat up and stretched. Her long time abed had left her stiff and weak. Renna helped her to stand. The girl who had brought Kila's supper the night before stood by holding a black robe.

"Your gown," the girl said in a whisper.

Kila waved it away. "I want *my* clothes."

Sens Renna said, "When the Voluptuary says you may have them, they will be returned to you."

Kila didn't like being naked in front of these people. And she hated being told what she had to wear. Besides, she didn't plan on staying at the Baths.

She snatched the garment from the girl's hands and pulled it over her head. It was very sheer. "I can almost see through it."

"And I can almost see through you," Renna said. There was no bitterness in her words. "You are uncomfortable being seen?"

Kila went to the door. It opened into a quiet hallway—walls of brick, whale oil lanterns. Incense smoked in a niche next to Kila's door, lifting a spicy sweet smell into the air.

She went right. The Sensual did not follow her. The doors along the way were unlocked. A few rooms were occupied. Two held boys wearing gowns just like Kila's. They sat on the edges of their cots, eyes half-closed, mouths curled in slight smiles. Neither looked at Kila when she barged in.

The third room was empty, but there was evidence that someone lived there. A book, an empty cup, a spare filmy dress. She opened the book. The Theb. The holy book of the New Pantheon. Kila's father had read to her from it when she was very small. He'd taught her to read the stories, always admonishing her that the gods were an invention. She was to enjoy the stories, but not believe in them. "Once you start believing in things, you surrender your mind to them," Father had said.

Kila left the room. The hallway ended here. She went the other direction. Renna stood in her doorway and watched as Kila stalked past.

More rooms. Three more boys and two girls. None of them looked at Kila when she walked in. They were all in the same weird trance.

No windows. The sense of being underground bothered Kila. She felt trapped.

Nax? she sent.

No reply.

This stretch of the hall ended at the bottom of a wooden staircase. She started up, taking them two at a time. She heard Renna following, though slowly.

The stairs opened into another hallway. More rooms. Some occupied, some not. Everyone was young and dressed in the same simple frock. The same incense burned in niches on this level.

Another staircase opened into a high-ceilinged hall bright with sunlight. Two enormous circular stained-glass windows stood opposite each other.

"The one on the left is the Sunrise Rose," Renna said, stopping behind Kila. "You will enjoy its glories many times in the years to come. The one on the opposite wall is the Sunset Rose."

Light flowed through the patterns of colored glass in each of the windows, filling the space with blues and reds and greens. Benches stood in rows before each of the windows. A wide aisle separated them.

Kila could only imagine what the windows must look like with a rising or setting sun behind them. Glorious, she supposed. The windows were ten spans wide at least.

"You'll notice there is no altar here," Renna said. "Ori does not wish to be glorified. She wishes us to glory in the sensations of life. Soon you will feel the Sensual mercus and know ecstasies both small and great. You will know that grief and pain and love and pleasure are all part of one great feeling."

Kila narrowed her gaze and regarded the handsome woman. The windows colored Renna's white hair a blur of orange and red.

"I'll not spend more time here than it takes to open yon door."

A new voice rose in the room. "When you can open the door, you may leave."

It was the Voluptuary. She stood in front of a tapestry on the rear wall. Kila hadn't seen her come in. The woman still wore her robe of many layers. Three men and three women stood behind her, all in the same kind of robe. Two of the men were clean-shaven, and the other one had a thick gray beard flowing down his front.

The women were dark-skinned, with flat faces and round eyes. They were from Iops, the island realm in the southern sea of Vichla. Kila had seen few of such folk in her life so she was amazed to see three at once, all so similar-looking they might have been sisters. Kila squinted. They *were* sisters, she decided.

The Voluptuary strode forward, hands clasped and resting against her belly. "The Sensuals of Ori do not like to take prisoners. But you are a danger to yourself and others in your current state."

"And what state might that be?" Kila asked. She eyed the door, then the strange group. They all watched Kila with calm interest. All wore the same half-smile.

"Untrained, and coming into the Sensual mercus on your own." The Voluptuary removed something from a slit pocket in her robes. Kila could not see what it was. The woman held the object in her fist. "What am I holding, Kila Sigh?"

"Are we playin' at riddles?"

"Stop with the Cheaps. What am I holding?"

"A magic ring. One that makes ya invisible."

The Voluptuary laughed through her nose. The men and women behind her smiled at each other.

"What I hold is not from a children's story about dwarves and halflings. Use the Sensual mercus, Kila. *See* what I hold."

Kila considered making a run for it. With light coming in through the rose windows, she at least knew she was above ground. All she had to do was find an unlocked door.

Assuming she could reach one. Nobody present seemed to be armed. But that didn't mean they couldn't hurt her. The Sensuals could use the mercus. She'd heard stories of the towers of flame the Donse Masters summoned in wars ages past. Perhaps those tales were exaggerated, but Kila didn't much want to risk a singeing of her nearly naked hindquarters.

She ambled forward, squinting at the Voluptuary's hand as if she really was trying to look.

"If you run, you will be stopped." The Voluptuary's voice was matter of fact. To support the claim, a figure emerged from a corner.

It was Yiqa, the Alnassi woman. She stood near the door, arms folded across her chest. Her scarf was down, letting her hair flow free. It was more gray than Kila expected, but nothing in the woman's posture spoke of advanced age.

The Voluptuary raised her voice. "The Sensual mercus, child. Do not name what you see. Merely allow your eyes to see *what is.*"

Kila understood that last bit. That was how she saw metals, by relaxing her vision and seeing the world without naming what she saw.

"I don't feel it at the moment," Kila said.

"You don't feel what?"

"The thing where I hear everything and smell everything and feel like I've drunk one beer too many."

The Voluptuary turned her head slightly. "Sens Goolsoy, if you please."

The man with the white beard stepped forward. His round belly led the way. Veins stood out on the backs of his gnarled hands. There was strength in them. Given his stature, Kila imagined the man would be more at home wearing breastplate than in these strange robes.

Sens Goolsoy smiled at Kila, lips pressed together, eyes crinkling. He spoke in a resonant baritone. "The feeling you describe. It mean you resist Sensual mercus."

"I don't resist it. It just comes over me when there's danger."

"Your mind too cluttered with thought. You not command your attention." Goolsoy held up a thick finger. "Danger focus mind, allow Sensual mercus to rise."

Kila smirked and nodded at the Voluptuary's hand which still concealed some mysterious item. "If you want me to do the metal trick, I'll need to get worked up about something. Maybe bring that Alnassi woman over to beat me bloody again."

Goolsoy did not react. He merely placed a hand on her forehead. "Focus attention on my touching."

Kila let out a weary sigh. The man's hand was very warm. His touch was gentle, just as Renna's was. His breath whistled in his nose. He closed his eyes. A warm smell wafted from him—like Nax's fur after the cat been lying in a patch of sun.

"You not focus," he said.

Kila rolled her eyes. "I feel yer paw on my head. What more focus d'ya want?"

"Feel press of hand. Feel heat. My skin, your skin.

This is essence of Sensual mercus. Close eyes. Feel contact."

Kila closed her eyes. Goolsoy's hand pressed against her forehead, a patch of warmth covering both eyebrows and up to her hairline. There was a bit of give to his flesh, which was dry.

"You no feel light head this time," he said, voice a whisper. "All senses awake! Now. You smell tea I spilled on robes this morning."

It was true. She did smell it. A blend called Hard Black, common in every Starside kitchen. The smell became so strong that Kila *tasted* the bitter brew on the back of her tongue.

"Hear mantra Sens Renna recite now."

There it was, as if whispered into Kila's ear. "The glories of flesh and spirit are the gifts of Ori. I receive pleasures, I give pleasures. I receive pains, I accept pains."

Goolsoy's hand grew hotter, like the midday sun on her forehead. The filmy gown draping over Kila's shoulders came alive, every thread caressing her where it touched. The stone floor was cool and rough on her bare feet.

This was the zing, Kila realized. But without the strange sense of space in her mind. This was the world as it was, unresisted.

"Voluptuary has what in hand?" Goolsoy whispered as he pulled his paw from her head.

Kila turned her eyes to the woman's hand. She

allowed her vision to relax, and finally it did. There was no woman before her, just shapes and colors and sounds and smells, unnamed. This was the Voluptuary as she was.

Metals sprang into view, glowing as bright and colorful as sunlight passing through the Sunrise Rose.

The Sensuals behind her wore no metal save their hair pieces, which were silver. The door across the hall had iron hinges and a strange latch that glowed blue. Kila did not recognize what alloy it was.

The thin metal binding that separated sections of colored glass in the two Rose windows hazed darkly with the distinct mercus signature of lead. Through the walls, shining dimly, were the downspouts of neighboring buildings.

Kila looked at the Voluptuary's hand.

The small object she concealed glowed white. A high-pitched resonance accompanied the glow, like a small bell infinitely ringing.

Kila stepped closer. Then closer still.

"What do I have in my hand?" the Voluptuary asked.

"It *is* a ring," Kila said. "I don't recognize the metal."

The woman opened her hand. The glow intensified the closer Kila got. The bell-like resonance grew louder.

"Take it, child."

Kila held it up. It was heavy, considering how small it was.

"What is the metal?" Kila asked, enraptured by the beauty of the glow and the pure tone of its resonance.

"No one knows."

Another voice rose, this one female and accented in the slurred way of Iops. "The wood, Voluptuary?"

The woman took the ring from Kila's hands and put it in her pocket. She removed another object and concealed it in her hand.

"What do I hold in my hand?"

Kil looked, but only saw the shape of woman's aged fingers closed in a loose fist.

"I can only see your hand."

The Voluptuary put the object away and brought out a flask. "What is in the vessel?"

The flask was pewter. Something caught at her mind as she sought to see inside the flask. An instinct more than a thought told her not to seek the same sort of cue as she received from metals. She closed her eyes and inhaled through her nose.

All the smells of the room came to her, each distinct. She could focus on Goolsoy's tea stain or she could focus on the Voluptuary's breath, which told of fruit. Apples.

The flask was sealed, but it didn't matter. Kila smiled. "Trezz. I never woulda thought an upright lady such as yerself would imbibe the loose juice."

This brought snickers from the others.

"Well done, Kila Sigh. Now, if you want to leave, open the door."

Still full of the zing, Kila went to the door. Yiqa stepped aside, though she did not seem happy to do so.

Using her mercus vision, Kila saw the latch was a simple bolt mechanism inside the door frame. The tumblers of the lock were lined up in a barrel embedded into the door. But there was no keyhole.

And a thick door it was. She counted at least fifteen tumblers, though there were several gaps where a tumbler appeared to be missing.

"You perform mercus feat," Goolsoy said from behind her. "Not simple, but you have strength."

Kila had no idea what he was talking about. She could see metal, and sniff out liquids maybe, but *using* the mercus? That was the domain of Donse Masters, not Cheapsgate thieves.

And yet something thrilled in her at the thought of doing it. Who was she to tell these people she couldn't unlock a keyless door if they thought she could?

Except she had no idea how to do it.

"I do not expect you to succeed," the Voluptuary whispered. "Merely to show you what you must learn."

Kila went closer, placed a hand on the door. It was heavy, oak. The surface was smooth with varnish, the surface cool. A brass handle jutted from it. Four mighty brass hinges, each plate as thick as Kila's pinky, connected the door to a wooden frame set into the stone wall.

Kila knew locks. Wen kept their father's pick set, not that it would help her here. Despite her frustration with being made a prisoner, she realized with amazement how easy it would be to pick a normal lock if she learned to access the mercus vision at will.

The vision was needed here, too. One would have to see the tumblers to move them.

Kila? Nax's voice broke into her thoughts. The cat was very far away.

I'm here. Where are you?

The sewers. I found Lop. I'm glad you are awake.

Me, too. I was sleeping like Mayla in the Egg.

You were dark.

A hand pressed onto Kila's shoulder, turned her. Goolsoy. "Come. You train now."

Kila pulled away from the man and turned back to the door, pretending to study it.

There is a way out, Kila sent. *It's a test of my skill with the mercus.*

Nax took a few seconds to reply. *Then I will not expect to see you for a long time.* The longing in Nax's sending made sadness bloom in Kila's chest. Nax sent, *Henley and Huff were going to rescue you, but Huff says Henley was captured.*

Captured. By who?

Nax didn't answer. A feeling of emptiness came through the connection. Absence.

I miss you, kitty. I'll get out as soon as I can. How is Wen?

He has used up his medicine and coughs all the time. Fallo seeks Finta Sahng.

Good. Do you have any idea where she is?

Fallo has tracked a rumor to people in the sewers.

The thinnies?

Yes. Them.

Be careful, Naxie. They cannot be trusted.

Who can be?

A fair enough question. And in truth, Kila did not trust Fallo would find Finta, certainly not if they had to deal with thinnies to do it. The boy was a runaway, and not wise in the ways of life. Not compared to her, anyway.

She dropped her chin slightly and whispered, knowing the Voluptuary would hear. "I need to leave now."

"I showed you the door," the Voluptuary whispered back.

"Open it for me. My brother needs my help."

"He will have to look after himself. He has those two boys. They have their cats."

The ache in Kila's chest flared hotter. More anger than ache. "One of the boys knows where your sister is." Not exactly true, but Kila didn't think she owed the Voluptuary the truth.

"Tell me."

Kila turned and spoke clearly. "That isn't how

deals work. I give you something of value, you give me something of value."

"You want me to release you. But your safety is more important than Finta's. It is more important than your brother's health." The Voluptuary's voice did not betray any concern for her sister. Maybe she was putting on a good face for the others.

"My safety is my concern, not yours."

The Voluptuary whispered, but Kila's zinged ears heard the words clearly. "I cannot let you fall into the Hargothe's hands. You'll end up in a cell, bound to a mercus chain, earning your supper by powering mercus lights for a Radiant in Gristenside. If you're lucky."

Kila knew that the Way of Til provided such services to those wealthy enough to pay. But the acolytes themselves . . . She'd assumed they did it out of devotion to their Way.

"I can see the confusion on your face, child. Why would the Way of Til waste the mercus talents of even one person to create light for a rich Radiant? I'll tell you only that there are reasons. None of them concern you."

"Send Yiqa, then," Kila whispered. "With her help, Fallo might get Finta free."

The boy would hate having to cooperate with Yiqa, but he might not get killed if he had the Alnassi woman's fighting skills on his side.

"I don't send Yiqa anywhere. I explain my needs and she decides whether she can and will help."

Yiqa's face was hard, eyes narrow. Kila knew the look. Yiqa had not heard the entire conversation. That meant she had not followed the whispered portion. She did not have the mercus.

Interesting.

Kila turned toward the Alnassi woman. "The Voluptuary's sister has been snatched up by the thinnies. My friend has the trail."

The woman's chest inflated as she drew an angry inhalation. Yes, she was loyal to the Voluptuary. And she was incensed that someone would kidnap the woman's sister.

"I cannot ask you to go, Yiqa," the Voluptuary said. "It is not a matter for the Way of Ori."

"You neet not asssk. I go." Her eyes shifted to Kila. "Tell mmmeee."

Kila sent to Nax, *The woman who beat me like a Tilsday rug-thrashing is coming to help Fallo find Finta Sahng. Tell him to meet her at the Cherry Hill sewer grate. Tell Fallo to let her help.*

Fallo says no.

Tell Fallo I said he can sleep on the roof of the Warren.

Fallo says we will meet her at the grate.

Goolsoy was smiling, his beard hopping with a silent chuckle. "You talk to cat?"

Kila wondered how the man knew. A question for another time. Finta needed Yiqa's help. Now. "Yiqa, there is a sewer grate at the bottom of Cherry Hill. It is in an alcove behind the Inn."

The woman nodded and marched away. Kila watched with great interest as the deadly woman descended the stairs Kila had come up. So, there was another exit that way. Somewhere.

Using her mercus vision Kila followed the woman's blade, which shined with a bluish white light of its steel. Kila wanted to run after and see how Yiqa escaped the building, but the Voluptuary's followers had moved to bar the stairway.

"It pains me to say it, but you folk aren't slow in the brain," Kila said.

"Do you think you are the first novitiate to realize there is more than one exit from this place?"

Goolsoy chuckled again. "I went on roof. Made rope from bed linens. Tied on Ori's Mark. Fell." He made a whistling noise and plopped his hands together.

"And I found him on the street below," the Voluptuary said, smiling at the reminiscence. "Broken leg and a bloody nose."

"Spent ten-day penance. Wash clothes. Scrub pots."

Kila smirked at the Voluptuary. "There's no chance in Kil's kitchen that you were the Voluptuary back then."

"I'm no fresh-hatched atlen, child," the Voluptuary said.

Kila had the distinct feeling the woman was

making sport of her. Kila decided not to reward such behavior with looking as embarrassed or confused as she felt.

"I won't try to escape," Kila said, "if you promise my clothes and my coins and my blade are somewhere safe."

"They are safe and will be returned to you the day you open that door."

Something about the promise bothered Kila. It struck her, then. "I am going to say something that'll probably get me into it deep. But I can't help it. I'm my father's daughter."

"Out with it," the Voluptuary said.

"I reckon not a one of you can open this door."

This brought a humorless smile to the Voluptuary's face. The women and men behind her lost their half-smiles.

"Goolsoy, I leave her in your capable hands." The woman departed through a door Kila had not noticed before, as it was hidden behind a tapestry.

The three Iopsi women trailed after. The remaining two men descended the same stairs Yiqa had gone down.

That left Kila alone in the Rose Hall with Goolsoy. He clasped his hands behind his back. The humor had drained out of his face, replaced with the serious mien of an impending lecture. Kila was already bored with it.

"You plan sneak around promise," Goolsoy said.

"Marnie heard every lie before. She know. You try leave first chance you get."

"Who is Marnie?"

"Voluptuary. We novitiates together long time ago. Partner. You have partner, too. Together, partner practice lesson. Together, you live. Together, succeed or fail. Together, reward or punish."

Kila did not like the sound of this at all. "I work best by myself, Sens Goolsoy."

"You have team of thieves."

"That's different."

Goolsoy dropped the subject. "Sensual mercus eludes you. Why?"

"I feel it right now," she said, unwilling to concede his point, correct though it may be.

"Sensual mercus fade. You no focus when you want." He flourished his hand and a gold skillet appeared in his fingers.

He smiled at her eyes brightening. "Ah. Now focus easy."

Kila liked the look of gold, especially coins. "That would pay off Parlo Odok. It could buy Wen his medicine."

The man moved the coin back and forth. Kila watched it.

"Your attention awake now. If you starve and see bread, greater awake."

Kila saw the truth of what he said, but she was still not willing to grant any part of his argument. She knew cons who tricked people into giving their money away using the very same technique. Tricky words were Kil's tongue in men's mouths.

The coin went back into the folds of Goolsoy's gown and out came a wooden stick. A twig off a tree.

"This object boring," Goolsoy said, waving it around like a fairytale wand. "Until I make interesting."

Light bloomed from the end of the stick, white and piercing. Kila stepped back, shielding her eyes with a hand.

The flare of light faded. Kila blinked, still seeing a blotch of color.

"The Sensual mercus!" Goolsoy said, tapping the stick on his palm. "I teach you. Some day. First you learn focus attention on boring thing."

"How does making light help me unlock that door?"

The man nodded slowly. "Open door harder than make light. But same thing. Focus—focus center of all. Call it Sensual mercus because must focus *senses*."

Kila caught the thread he seemed to be dangling. "Light is focused sight, isn't it? And hearing? Can you make sounds with the mercus?"

A bell rang, high up in the room.

"Indeed." Goolsoy was panting now. He drew up two layers of his flimsy gown and mopped his glistening forehead. Kila was glad he had several more layers to keep himself covered.

"And odors?"

"You smell terrible things when novitiates learn skill. Pranksters. Create smell not only thing Sensual mercus do."

He clamped his lips together and closed his eyes. Sweat beaded on his face, ran down his nose. His breath whistled in and out, like a man carrying a great weight uphill.

Kila felt herself soften toward the man. He had a nice face, she thought. Grandfatherly. She had never known either of her grandfathers. She hadn't known her mother either. She had a sudden urge to hug Goolsoy.

He opened his eyes. "You feel warmth. Affection. Aspect of smell few know. Use mercus attention. Notice now."

The glow of metals had faded. But Kila's heightened senses remained, the zing without the light-headed feeling. She breathed in. Goolsoy smelled soapy and the tea stain still had that bitter edge. "Nothing different."

"Relax smell."

She caught on. It was like relaxing her vision to see the metals. She needed to stop naming the odors around her. She closed her eyes and tested the air. There *was* something else there. An odor, but not one that smelled like anything. It smelled like a feeling.

A charm.

Now that Kila knew it was happening, she felt

some of the affection recede. Goolsoy was just an old man. And one she was not happy to be too near. If he could create that feeling in her, what other feelings might he be tempted to plant?

"No fear," he said, sensing her trepidation. "Cannot make you feel what you no feel. Mercus allure very subtle. Awaken what already there."

Kila backed away, still not trusting him. "Don't use taste on me. Or touch, neither."

"Touch . . . difficult. I too tired." He raised the stick again. "Touch focus heat, or sap heat. Touch make pleasure. Make pain. Touch move object or hold object firm. Very powerful. *Very* difficult."

If Goolsoy was this exhausted from his demonstrations so far, it meant unlocking the door might be beyond his abilities entirely. So Kila had been right.

"Great feats require many practitioner. All work like partner. You have task now."

"And that is?"

"Explore. Learn escape not possible. After, return to bedroom. Find partner there."

"You're telling me to escape?"

"No. I tell you *try*. Else, you too distracted by escape thought." Goolosy didn't wait for her to agree before going to the tapestry. "Try follow."

With that he pulled aside the tapestry and passed into the dim hallway beyond. The hanging fell back into place, the depiction of Til bearing the boulder on his back rippling like the surface of the sea before finally falling still.

Kila reached the tapestry in three long strides. Grasping the edge, she pulled it back.

No hallway. Just smooth stone wall. She rapped it with her knuckles. Solid.

She searched the base of the wall for a latch. Nothing.

Relaxing her vision, she sought out the glow of metal. A faint glimmer of brass shone through the wall. A sconce, she guessed. So, there *was* a hallway there. It had to require some trick of the mercus to get through. Just like the door.

She moved back to the center of the Rose Hall. It was very still in the great hollow space. Too still. With her senses enlivened, she should hear activity on the streets outside. The glass of the rose windows was not so thick as to block it all.

"So that's how it is," she said to whoever was listening. "Silencing things to hide secrets from me."

Someone *was* listening, she knew. Maybe one of those Iopsi ladies. If they all could go into the zing whenever they wanted, she assumed they'd do it all the time. They had certainly done something to create this unnatural silence in the Hall.

"I'm goin' downstairs!" she called, then started down the steps.

13

WAKE UP, FLEABAG

Backtracking to the grate at Cherry Hill irritated Fallo. But not being a complete idiot, he saw the value in allying with the Alnassi woman. How Kila had managed to dispatch her own kidnapper to assist him was one of those Kila-shaped mysteries Fallo decided better to ignore. Best to not question what couldn't be explained. This included—generally speaking—everything women said or did.

So far he hadn't seen any thinnies, which suited him just fine. Lop had scented out some evidence of them. And then, unexpectedly, Nax had joined them. The little gray now sat near Fallo's feet, tail primly wrapped around her white socks. Lop was asleep, of course.

Wake up, fleabag, he sent.

Food time?

No. But you're embarrassing me in front of Nax.

You should be embarrassed even when Nax is far away.

That's it. I'm cutting your food until you liven up.

That's it. I'm ignoring you until you feed me.

Fallo didn't get the last word, for the grate pulled back and the Alnassi woman dropped through. She landed like a cat. Only her eyes were visible in the gloom. The rest of her was all wrapped in black.

"You couldn't use the ladder?" he asked.

"Latter isss ssslow." She marched away.

Fallo went after her, Nax at his heels. Lop rose, stretched, and then moseyed along far behind.

Catching up to the woman, Fallo jerked his thumb over his shoulder. "Lop—that fat fuzzball behind us—found some of the thinnies' crumbs ahead. Maybe some atlen dung, too. But as Lop constantly reminds me, she's no bloodhound."

"Sshow mee."

It wasn't far. The Alnassi woman knelt in the spot Lop had found. Nax slinked closer to Fallo but stayed well away from the woman.

"You have a name, Alnassi?" Fallo asked.

She didn't look up. She stroked the wood plank walkway with her fingers, sniffed the air. The thinnies installed the walks to keep from having to slosh through the ankle-deep muck at the bottom of the tunnel. What the woman could possible see in this gloom was beyond Fallo.

"I ammm Yeekha," she said. "You aarre Faalloh."

"So what did you do with Kila and Henley?"

"Kila witt Sssenssuals. Do nnot know ozzer nname."

"Henley was looking for Kila. Then he went quiet. I think you knocked him out and stuffed him in a barrel."

"No. Thisss waay." She continued down the tunnel. Fallo didn't find her tracking skills especially impressive, considering there was no other choice. Nax kept well back from her. Lop ambled along far behind, stopping to nose anything that might be edible.

Any word from Huff? he sent to Lop.

The cat didn't answer.

I'll give you a hunk of cheese.

No word from Huff. Huff is trying to get in.

Get in where?

Cheese.

Fallo reached into a pouch and pinched off a corner of soft cheddar. Lop darted up to him and gobbled it down.

Get in where? Fallo asked again.

I don't know. A place.

What does it look like?

Buildings.

Will you tell me if Huff tells you more?

Maybe.

Fallo gave up on the conversation. Surely if Huff found something of use, Lop would pass it on.

Probably.

Hopefully.

14

HEALTHY MAN WHEN HE DIED

I ncense burned from seventeen golden censers placed in burners mounted on columns surrounding the nave of the Cathedral of Til. Each coil of shanlán incense cost ten gold skillets. They would burn day and night for the Choosing Fast, during which the Nare Donse Masters debated which of them would become Highest of Til.

The tendrils of coppery smoke wound to the arched ceiling, where they formed a thick haze. The intricate gilded decorations that covered the cupola were barely visible. The windows circling it were kept closed. The doors were chained shut.

The Hargothe lay upon a bed near the altar. He wasn't a Nare, so he did not have a vote. His presence served only as pressure to force the assembled fools to come to an agreement. Hunger would do most of the work. The Hargothe did not need to see the men to know how rotund many of them had grown. It was a truism among the masses that a Donse Master would always be found near a full pantry and a fat purse. One did not rise to the rank of Nare without mastering the intrigues of politics. Such skills favored those who were not shy in pursuing their own hungers.

At the moment Nare Fillus was rambling on about the qualities he desired in a Highest. Of course, he merely summarized his own accomplishments and character. The Hargothe noted the man did not once mention piety among the requisite qualities.

The Hargothe's nose twitched as a smell reached him. Bacon. It came from Nare Fillus's flapping lips. The man had secreted some food in his robes, no doubt. No wonder he maintained the strength to keep up his incessant harangues.

Many of the Nare slept on the floor. No chairs were permitted during the Choosing. Chamber pots were allowed, fortunately. Though the men tried to be conscientious about their bodily needs, a day's worth of their eliminations stewed in casks tucked in one of the side chapels.

It was a testament to how greedy the Nare were for power that they had not yet come to agreement despite the deprivations imposed upon them by the laws of the Way.

The Hargothe wished he could be deprived of the stink and incessant noise these men emitted. He almost regretted deposing Nare Chilow. But the man had let Kila Sigh fall into the grasp of the Harlots of Ori.

He could feel her even now. She had come alive upon the mercusine suddenly and very brightly within the last hour. That after a long absence. It would be better if she were dead than in the hands of those lascivious tarts.

But no. That wasn't true. He could still have her.

First, he must end this farce of a Choosing. He rang his bell.

Nare Fillus stopped speaking as all eyes turned toward the Hargothe. A warble of fear came across the mercus as the lesser Nares failed to conceal their emotions. He fought the temptation to sweep into their minds and plant his decision. They'd know he'd intruded, and that would invalidate their votes. That would have the opposite effect of what he wanted.

This called for a more subtle—and paradoxically—more direct approach.

He beckoned to Nare Fillus. *Come to me.*

A hush fell over the men until there only remained the sound of Fillus's soft shoes scraping the mosaic floor of the cathedral. The steps grew louder, the man's robes adding an irritating swish to his movements.

"Do you need assistance, Seer Hargothe?" the Nare asked.

The Hargothe chose his words carefully. "What

was the last count?" He knew the last count, but he needed to guide Fillus to the correct conclusion.

"Forty-nine for Nare Wiles. Thirty for Nare Extemp, and twenty-one for me."

The count hadn't changed by more than two votes in as many hours. Nare Wiles was a buffoon, who bought votes with promises of future favors. He'd be subject to blackmail the very day he donned the vestments of the Highest. Nare Extemp was wise, but had said a dozen times he would not accept the position unless it was unanimous. Nare Fillus merely wanted the majority, but his penchant for lectures being well-known, nobody wanted to endure a single Tilsday with him at the pulpit, let alone a ten-year.

"Throw your support to Nare Binel."

"But Seer, he is so young."

Barely in his third ten-year, Binel was also weak-minded, venal, and greedy. And every Nare of experience thought they could use him.

Do it and Til shall reward you.

"How?"

The Hargothe noted that Fillus didn't question the truth of his statement. The Hargothe was a Seer, after all. The man took his words as prophecy.

I see a throne of gold and you upon it. He saw no such thing.

"A throne, you say?" The man's voice swaddled the idea with loving avarice. "Til is great."

Til is wise.

The Nare turned away from the Hargothe and moved to the edge of the altar dais. "I throw my support to Nare Binel."

A chorus arose as the Nares murmured and gasped. The sharper minds saw what they thought was Fillus's scheme. Binel was like a flag atop a watchtower, flapping with the wind. Why be the flag when one could be the wind?

Each Nare thought he had the leverage or persuasion to sway Binel to their agenda. None did. Binel was the Hargothe's man. No one else's.

The vote was taken. All of Extemp's and Fillus's votes went to Binel, giving him the majority needed. The young Nare stood bewildered as the count was read. He carried it by one vote, leaving silly Nare Wiles to grouse of plots and schemes.

Count yourself lucky, Wiles, the Hargothe said into the man's mind. *Highest Chilow was a healthy man when he died.*

Hargothe summoned his servants to move him to his crypt sanctuary. After his body had been washed and oiled, and once he'd swallowed a portion of bland gruel, he instructed his elderly servant to pass a word to the new Highest.

"I have work for him to do."

15

MY PARTNER

The Baths of Ori had to encompass more than the Rose Hall and the initiates' wards below it. Kila was stuck in one building of many. She knew that because she'd seen the compound from the bell tower.

The problem was getting outside. She went into every room, again seeing the novitiates in their weirdly happy trances. She searched the privies and the baths at the end of the halls.

A dim library with three tiers of musty bookshelves occupied a central area accessible by a somewhat hidden spiral staircase. Overstuffed leather chairs and dark-stained wooden tables huddled in a central reading area. Thick carpets covered the stone floor. It would have been cozy if the ceilings hadn't been so high and dark.

Nobody was there, and the hearth of a great fireplace was cold.

Seeing the countless books made Kila think of her father. He had loved to read. Kila hadn't had much chance to practice recently. The old copy of the Theb father had taught her to read from had been lost long ago. She'd read it so many times she'd gotten bored with it. Besides, she didn't believe any of the stories in it. She preferred the tales of Kil. They weren't written down, but oldsters would tell them if you got them a little trezzed first.

She considered swiping a few of the books once she found a way out. Books were valuable. She could read them then sell them.

But first she had to escape. She wandered back up to Rose Hall, stumped. There were no doorways out of the building, aside from the keyless main door and that passage behind the tapestry.

It didn't make any sense. Why would access to the entire compound—and presumably the baths themselves—go through the tapestry? And Yiqa had gone down those steps. For that matter, so had two of the male Sensuals.

The other doors had to be hidden. No amount of staring or sniffing with her mercus-enlivened senses showed her a hint of a way out. She even looked for wear patterns on the hallway floors to see if they led to where a door should be.

Nothing.

She returned to the spot where Sens Goolsoy showed her his tricks with light and smell and sound. She recalled his story about attempting escape from the roof. Kila kept the smile off her lips, though she thrilled inside. Sens Goolsoy had gotten onto the roof. That's where he tied his makeshift rope to Ori's Mark and climbed down. He'd broken a leg.

Rooftops were Kila's favorite place to be. If Sens Goolsoy could get up there, so could she. Her eyes fell on the Sunset Rose. Windows. The Roses wouldn't open. But other windows would.

Just as quickly as her heart leapt in hope, it crashed in despair. There were no windows in the novitiates' ward.

Kila chewed her lower lip as she puzzled over this conundrum. She didn't have long to think about it, for a striking young man appeared at the top of the stairs. He wore the same type of filmy gown as Kila. She was relieved to see that it wasn't as sheer as she had feared.

He had a mess of blond curls atop his head. A few locks tumbled over his left eye. Pausing at the entrance to Rose Hall, he watched her with the unmistakable air of someone who would rather meet anyone else.

She knew him.

"You?" they both said at the same time.

His voice was not as quavery as Kila had remembered. In his defense, she had been robbing him the first—and last—time they'd met.

"Ill met, lordling," she said, giving a mock bow. "I'm guessing you're not keen on finding me here."

"On the contrary. I have been looking forward to this day." He rubbed his jaw, as if remembering how she'd shoved his cheek onto the paving stones beneath the Harridan Gate. "You owe me two gold for the cat you stole."

Kila pinched the sides of her frock and gave a short tug to the sides to show her non-existent pockets. "Were you working for the Senuals when you had Oly in that sack?"

He went to a bench along the aisle and sat. His shoulders were broad, but a bit boney. His figure was slight, though he stood a head taller than Kila. She found his mouth irritating, the way it held a haughty smile even at rest. "I presume Oly is the cat? Never mind. I'd rather not know. But to answer your question, I was not working for the Voluptuary."

"So why does a rich Keel need to rack off a cat for two gold skillets?" Kila had tailed the drunken young man through the wee-hours' quiet of the merchant quarter. She'd had to fight off Fallo and Henley, who'd been stalking the man, too. That was before the two boys had become family. In the end, she'd taken this lordling's empty purse and the mysterious sack he'd carried. That sack had contained Oly.

"My father disowned me. I'd rather not say why.

The bounty I would have received for the cat was going to pay off some rather pressing debts. After you robbed me, I had no recourse but to seek sanctuary here."

"The Donse Masters wouldn't have you?"

The young man spluttered with laughter. "You think *they* offer haven from debtors? Perhaps you'd be better off hanging flowers around the neck of Mayla in a countryside spring festival. You're as naive as they come."

The Way of Ori did not pay debts, but merely offered protection. In return, they expected a lifetime of devotion

"You have a name, Keel?" she asked.

"Raginalt. My friends call me Ragin." He pronounced it "rage-in."

"So I'll call you Raginalt."

"And you are Kila Sigh. The Cheapsgate waif I've heard so much about from Sens Goolsoy."

"My friends call me Kila," she said, smiling with only her mouth. "Everyone else calls me 'stop thief!'"

"You like that, don't you? Being called thief?"

"It's a noble calling."

"It's criminal."

Kila's father had taught her how to steal. She had never considered the right or wrong of it. She tried to take only from those who could spare it. If she had misidentified Raginalt as a rich lordling, it was his own fault. If one is up to one's eyeballs in debt, one should not stroll the streets drunk and with a cat in a sack.

"I heard you kept the cat you stole from me," he said.

"He belongs to my brother now."

"I thought you had a cat."

"I do."

"And? What is its name?"

Kila wasn't about to tell this young fool anything about her precious Naxie. "Is there some reason you ambled into this hall at this particular time of day?"

"Sens Renna said I'd find my partner here."

She blew out a hard breath. She was going to be saddled with this wool-brained bumblefoot. The Voluptuary probably arranged it to inconvenience Kila as much as possible.

Kila could see two options. The first was to ignore Raginalt entirely and hope he gave up. But he probably didn't have any more say in the matter than she did. The second option was to bring him around to her way of thinking and get him to help her escape.

"I don't suppose you happen to know how to get onto the roof of this hall," she said. "If you can get me there, you can be rid of me."

"The roof?" Raginalt stood up and clasped his hands. "I do, indeed."

"Well, tell me. I'll be on my way, and we don't have to waste more time pretending to be civil."

This evoked a genuine laugh from the boy,

showing one crooked tooth in a smile that was otherwise straight and white. In any other face, that defect might have been charming. In this case, Kila felt an impulse to punch him in the mouth.

"Pretending is the soul of civility," he said. It sounded like he was quoting someone else. "I can show you the way to the roof, but you won't like it."

"Liking things has never figured into my life, Raginalt Keel."

"Then come with me, Kila Sigh." He went back to the stairs, the hem of his gown swishing in his wake. It was like everyone was traipsing around in their nightshirts in this place.

He looked over his shoulder as they descended the stairs. "You must promise that you'll wash my clothes if you fail to escape."

"Why would I promise such a silly thing?"

"It isn't much, just this gown and one more like it. Do we have a deal?"

"Yes. Just bring the laundry to my room." She suppressed a snicker. If she could get to the roof, she'd be back to the Warren in less than an hour.

The thought pleased her until he answered. "Easily done, since we share a room here."

16

ACOLYTE'S ROBES

The cell smelled of an overflowing chamber pot.

Henley pressed his hands onto the floor. It was covered with a layer of very old straw, greasy with mud, and giving off a horrific stench. The darkness was absolute.

Henley's brain ached. There was no way his head was big enough to contain the depths in which he felt the pain.

Throat ragged and burning from thirst, he called out, "Hello? Where am I?" It came out in a whisper.

Huff?

No answer. He felt the cat's presence, far off and vague, as if Huff were asleep.

Waving his arms in front of himself, Henley explored his prison. A low, slanting ceiling kept him from standing upright. Arms extended, he could touch opposite walls. A thick wooden door filled most of one side. Not much more than a closet, and a very low one at that.

Fear penetrated the aches of his body. The air felt thick in his nostrils. He tried breathing through his mouth, but there didn't seem to be anything in the breaths. Panic fluttered across his skin, hot and prickly.

"Let me out. Please!" His dry throat cracked. His words fluttered, weak and useless.

He hammered on the door, rammed his shoulder into it, careless of the pain. Half screaming, half sobbing, he strove to break his way out. He might as well have tried to smash through bedrock. The door clunked, but didn't move by a hair.

The vigor of panic drained as quickly as it had arisen. He fell to the floor, breath heaving. There was no air. No sustenance. The darkness pressed against him as heavy as a mountain.

So this was death. Father and brother had met it before him. But he did not want to cross to Til's golden fields or to Kil's fiery chasm. What life had he lived yet? What was the purpose to have been born if to die like this?

Light seared his eyes, and clean air swept all around him. He drew in sweet breaths, pressing his hands to his eyes to block out the white fire.

"Can you stand, son?" A stern, but not unkindly voice.

He got to his feet, though his knees shook. Parting his fingers, he peered into the face of the same gray-haired Donse Master who had captured him. Dunne Qirl. The man held a wooden staff, the top glowing with mercus light.

Nearby was an elderly man in acolyte's robes. "Seer Hargothe requires your audience." The man spoke in such a low whisper, Henley barely heard him.

Henley only wanted out of the cell. Where they took him did not matter.

"First you must bathe," the old man said. "The Hargothe is sensitive to odors such as yours."

A bath sounded like a dream. But a new fear rose in him. Perhaps they had recognized him after all. Perhaps visiting this Seer person was prelude to being turned over to the Keels. He felt for his knit cap and was relieved to discover it still covering his distinctive ginger hair.

They led him to a plain, well-lit room containing a giant tub filled with steaming water. They did not leave him in privacy, but instead instructed him to soap and scrub himself raw. When he was done, he was given acolyte's robes.

He didn't care. These all seemed like good portents. Why have him clean up merely to be turned over to executioners? It seemed the Donse Master who had captured him truly believed he possessed mercus powers. What a disappointment they were in for.

They took him to another room, this one with a cot and nothing else. A small tray of bread and soup awaited him. The acolyte and Donse Master locked him in.

Henley fell on the food, eating like the ravenous creature he was.

Huff?

I'm here. Where are you?

Trapped.

Come out.

It might take some time.

17

YOUR LEGS, YOUR BACK, YOUR SKULL

Now Kila understood why Raginalt had been so sure she wouldn't like the way to the roof. And also why he'd exacted the promise that she'd wash his clothes.

The library fireplace was cold. She bent to peer up the flue. A tiny square of daylight shined at the top. The soot smell stung her nose and flakes of black dust made her sneeze. The chimney was narrow, but probably wide enough.

"Are we going up?" Raginalt asked, feigning cheer.

Again resisting the urge to hit the young man, Kila put her hands on her hips and considered the task of climbing up. It wouldn't be particularly difficult, but she would come out completely blackened.

She didn't see what choice she had. This was obviously the way Goolsoy had gone up all those years ago. A tickle in the back of her mind got her wondering if the old Sensual had mentioned his failed stunt just to get her to try it.

It didn't matter. She had to get out of here.

Nax? she sent.

She didn't expect a response. The cat felt very far from her. An ache in her chest pulsed along with her heartbeat. She needed to be close to her little gray friend, to feel the cat's soft ears against her cheek.

"Let's climb," she said. No need to think about it. The task was the task. Gritting her teeth, she bent under the mantel and straightened into the chimney. Bracing her back on one wall and her feet on the other, she started to inch her way up.

The light below her went dark as Raginalt came in after her. "Try not to fall on me," he said.

"Try not to look up my skirt."

All she got in reply was a wicked snicker. Fortunately, it was too dark in the sooty flue to see anything at all. Still, she kept grabbing the skirts of her thin gown and pulling them up between her legs.

"Why don't they give us something to wear under these frocks?"

"The breeze."

Kila noted the square of light above her was a bit larger now.

"That's it? The breeze? What does that mean?"

"Should be obvious. There's nothing between your nether regions and the breeze, is there?"

"That's a fact I cannot deny. But it isn't a *reason*."

"Goolsoy and Renna are Sensuals of Ori. The order is obsessed with the senses. Goolsoy told me that nakedness helps one focus on one's body. The gown conceals enough to prevent distractions. But I've heard there are rites performed by Sensuals done entirely in the nude."

Unwelcome images of Goolsoy and the Voluptuary popped into Kila's mind, quickly followed by a raised eyebrow as she considered what Raginalt might look like without his filmy gown. She banished the thoughts.

She decided not to respond to Raginalt's intentionally provocative statement. It was hard enough focusing on the climb; she didn't need him describing how the old folk were cavorting around in their skins.

The air freshened as she got to the chimney's opening. Finally climbing into the cool air, she took a deep breath. She blinked against the brightness of day, though the sun was hidden behind a skim of clouds. Thankfully, it wasn't raining.

She walked along the steeply-pitched roof to an edge looking over the wealthy Gristenside quarter. Greathouses set amidst vast green lawns sat well back from the Street of the Diadem, which was what rich folk called the Street of Sorrows. Smoke plumed from chimneys in gray wisps.

The bell tower she'd climbed with Nax stood on the opposite side of the compound. Behind her, the Divide loomed above all.

Kila immediately saw why Goolsoy had not been able to get down without a rope. The building she stood on was separated from its neighbors by a large span of emptiness on all sides. Far below lay tidy walkways trimmed with shrubs.

"What's that building?" Kila asked, pointing to the nearest roof. Like the one she stood upon, its roof was steeply-pitched. Not an ideal landing surface after a jump.

A *long* jump.

Raginalt inched beside her and looked over the edge. He swallowed and cleared his throat. "I'm a novitiate, just like you. I haven't been out of the ward until now. Unlike you, I don't see any advantage in escape."

Kila paced the roof of the Rose Hall, looking down on all sides. The front—where the mysterious door with no keyhole was—let out into a courtyard fronted by a gate that gave into the Street of the Diadem. The broad avenue continued south and slightly west as it wound through switchbacks climbing the slope toward the Citadel.

The bell tower stood to the east. It was attached to the temple where citizens came to ask Ori's blessings. The public baths were there.

She turned her eyes back to the shortest gap she'd have to jump. She studied the target roof and instantly saw the series of leaps and dives needed to get from it to the temple roof beneath the bell tower. From there, she'd be free.

"Surely you're not considering that jump," Raginalt said. "You'll break your legs, your back, and your skull."

Kila raised a brow and mocked his speech. "Surely you would not mind if I did."

She took three measured steps backward. The roof pitched down, so that would lend her some momentum. She gauged the drop to the ground was fifteen paces, and she'd have to cross six or so. If the target roof were the same height, she'd have no chance. But it was several paces lower, which would give her a jump a little more distance. She hoped.

The wooden shingles covering the other roof would punish her. And in this ridiculous outfit she'd have little protection from scrapes and bruises. If this were the roofway, she'd speak to a tenant about putting a landing pad on that roof.

But this was not the roofway.

She pictured the arc of her flight and realized that her gown would blow up over her head as she descended. Raginalt would surely get an unearned eyeful. That would not do.

She bunched the thin skirts in the front and back and hiked them up. A quick knot between her legs would keep the worst from happening, though it left her legs bare to the thigh.

Raginalt coughed, cheeks turning pink. "I do

believe you are seriously considering killing yourself. I implore you not to attempt this stunt."

She winked at him. "Thank you for the concern. But I have important business elsewhere."

Kila sprinted to the edge of the Rose Hall roof and leapt.

18

DEBACLE CATASTROPHE

Yiqa held up her hand, signaling Fallo to stop. They had walked a long way, slowly, with many stops for her to kneel, touch the ground, and sniff the air. Now they stood in a dark place, the last sewer grate far behind them sending beams of gray light into nothingness.

Fallo's eyes had adjusted as much as they could. Yiqa was a dark form in front of him. The cats huddled close to each other ten paces back. No fools they.

"Shall we continue or do you intend to stand like a statue forever?" Fallo whispered.

Yiqa slipped close to him, pressed her mouth to his ear. "Sommeone waits ahheadt."

Fallo did not know how Yiqa knew this, except that her senses were keener. Neither of the cats had sensed danger.

"So what do we do?"

"Wait."

A flutter of fabric and she was gone. Utterly. Not so much as a scuff of footfall told even which direction she went.

Knowing that someone was lying in wait did not comfort Fallo. In fact, he reflected that ignorance was always preferable to knowledge when it came to danger. A swift, unexpected death saved one much gut-churning fear.

Nervously he mouthed a snatch of verse that came to mind. "Jarek the brave faced the wyrm in its cave, yet he carried no blade, no maul, no flail. His courage none doubt, but he never came out, and all the remained was his mail." Fallo had always liked the Songs of Jarek, a hero so dimwitted he died at the end of every song. Now that Fallo was doing something similarly stupid, he had more sympathy for the lovable dolt.

How is Wen? he sent to Lop.

Wen is lying on his back.

Is he breathing?

Oly says you ask stupid questions.

And you agree?

Oly sees much that I do not, but on this we are united.

What about Kila and Henley?

Nax knows Kila lives. Nax wants to leave the sewers and return to where Kila is.

Tell Nax she's welcome to leave. Of course, climbing a

ladder and opening a sewer grate would be impossible for the small gray. For now, Kila's cat would have to stay with him.

And Henley? he asked.

Huff says Henley is not safe. We must help him. An uncharacteristic urgency accompanied Lop's words. The cat didn't seem to know how to convey what it felt.

Yiqa did not return. Fallo was worried about Henley. The lad was sharp as a Shadline blade, but inexperienced. Going off to find Kila had been necessary, but Fallo had known Henley's chances of success were slim. Whatever had happened to him had done something terrible to Huff. The cat didn't seem capable of communicating anything useful to Lop.

Fallo hoped Huff and Henley could manage to survive long enough for Fallo to come find them. Assuming he survived this current ridiculous situation.

His thoughts went to how he'd found Henley in the first place. He'd been prompted to search for someone in Cheapsgate by Her Enlightened herself. Not that she'd said it directly to him. The message had come on a blank card she'd sent to him when he'd visited the Citadel to present her a hermit's dagger. By Til's great and furrowed brow, did that adventure feel like a lifetime ago.

He worried that if something happened to Henley,

she would be angry with him. One did not want Her
Enlightened Majesty angry with them.

Footsteps sounded on the plank walkway ahead.
Yiqa appeared, a smoky apparition flying straight at
him. More footsteps resounded in the passage, these
heavier.

The Alnassi woman said nothing, but rammed into
Fallo and pushed him in the opposite direction. He
didn't need more encouragement.

Flames roared to life ahead and behind. Men and
women with torches blocked the way. A trap.

Thanks for the warning, Fallo sent to Lop.

I did not give you warning.

Of all the demaynic cats to be bonded with, Fallo
had ended up with one that did not understand
sarcasm.

Fallo stopped running, since going straight at thinnies didn't make sense to him. Yiqa did not stop. She
sprinted, angling at the center of the line. The cats
crouched low, tails flicking. Lop's fur stuck out in all
directions and she let out a warbling moan.

Yiqa took flight, tumbling through a series of hand-
springs and then launching over the thinnies' heads.
They turned to face her, the closest swinging flaming
brands like clubs. Yiqa avoided them with lunges that
flattened her to the floor yet kept her hands free. These
blurred with strikes to kneecaps, stomachs, and wrists.
One thinnie fell, then another. Seeing the opening,
Fallo ran.

He felt Lop speeding close by. Ahead, more thinnies dropped as Yiqa blurred among them, striking and tripping and kicking. Behind Fallo came a roar of outrage as those thinnies saw their quarry escaping.

Fallo burst past the remaining thinnies, who had now turned all their attention on Yiqa. Fallo sprinted for the light of the sewer grate and the ladder below it.

Unseen projectiles clattered near him, a few thunked into the planks of the walkway. The darts were tiny and backed by a fluffy white fletching. One dart brushed his hair. Another jerked the sleeve of his jacket. No sting.

Nax! Lop cried. Fallo stumbled as his cat's voice exploded in his head. He looked for Kila's small gray. Lop ran past him. Thinnies pounded closer, many holding tubes to their lips. They blew into them, producing *thoomps* of air. More darts struck at Fallo's feet.

He ran. *Where's Nax?*

Lost! Lost! Lost!

Where?

She has gone quiet like Huff. Lop's panic infected Fallo, and he strained to run faster. He faced a choice. Try to scramble up the ladder and hope he got above the range of thinnie blowpipes, or keep running and hope they gave up. He couldn't remember how far the next grate was. But he knew that he'd be even more exhausted by the time he reached it. Climbing a ladder then would be nearly impossible, especially with a crazed cat clinging to him.

He leapt onto the ladder, Lop simultaneously jumping to dig her claws into his jacket. Up she climbed, latching onto his shoulder. The terror she felt pulsed through Fallo's mind. It lent him strength. The rungs blurred in front of him as he climbed.

Something smacked into his pant leg. A dart. Another hit his shoe and fell away.

The square of light from the grate above grew. He threw his shoulder against it and it swung open. With a last burst of energy, he lunged into daylight and onto the street. Lop was already slinking into an alley.

Fallo slammed the grate shut and followed.

He stopped in the cover of the shadows to watch the grate. It didn't open.

Poor Nax, Lop sent.

What happened?

Captured. Put in a box.

Fallo stared at the grate a long time. He had failed to find Finta Sahng. He had lost Nax and Yiqa. There was no way he could face the thinnies in their own domain alone. It had been foolish to go down there at all.

We have to find Henley and Huff, he told Lop, plucking thinnie darts from his sleeve and pant leg. They were mere slivers of wood, the pointy end stained black. He sniffed and drew his nose away in disgust. "Smells like a sailor's arse."

Lop sent a sensation of fur being rubbed in the wrong direction, but she didn't argue. *This way to Huff.*

Fallo climbed to the roofway, and Lop led him up the slopes of Terriside.

They found Huff curled into a ball, hiding under a basket near the Harridan Gate. Fallo gingerly picked up the animal and tucked him into his jacket. Huff was breathing, his body warm, but no amount of jostling could stir more than a pathetic meow from him.

Where's Henley? he asked Lop.

Huff does not know. Huff is . . . not clear.

Let's get him back to the Warren. Then I'll go see Wen and discuss this debacle.

What's a debacle?

It's a catastrophe.

What's that?

It's the mess that happens when your friends go missing and their cats don't know where they went.

This is a debacle catastrophe.

As true as that?

Lop did not know the correct response, so Fallo answered himself. "As true as that."

19

WHAT VOW?

Kila's flight carried her for two long heartbeats. The target roof rose to meet her. Instinct took over. The practice of countless nights spent running and jumping, diving, landing, and rolling made her movements automatic.

Her feet struck the very edge of the roof. Momentum carried her head toward the shingles. She tucked and rolled, world spinning.

Her injured shoulder protested, sending white-hot lances of pain through her vision. All pretense of control escape her as she tumbled and bounced. The slope of the roof rolled her faster and faster toward the far ledge.

Desperate to stop, she spread her arms and legs. The skin of her bare thighs flamed as she skidded. Her toes jounced on the wood, picking up slivers and abrasions. Then her feet were in open air.

She jammed her palms onto the roof, scrabbling with fingertips to brake her movement. Finally, she stopped, her legs dangling over the drop. Her breath heaved in and out as she lay there. Pain kept her awake, though part of her mind longed for the solace of unconsciousness.

A thump and cry sounded nearby. She lifted her head in time to see Raginalt sliding toward her, his eyes wide.

With a swing of her legs, she scrambled onto the roof and threw her weight onto his. He grunted and cursed, but his body scraped to a stop.

"Yer an idiot, Ragin."

"Said the girl who jumped first."

"Who's dafter, the idiot who makes a wool-minded leap or the sheep that follows after?"

Ragin laughed through his moans of pain. "I cannot believe I did that. Ow."

Kila got to her feet, trembling. Her hands were raw again. Her knees wept droplets of blood. Her right cheek burned and a goose egg lump rose on the back of her head.

"That worked better than I expected," she said, putting on a brave tone for Ragin's benefit. In truth, she wanted to curl up and cry for a while.

She walked to the next ledge. "It'll be easier from here on."

Ragin stood and wiped a hand across his nose.

Blood dripped from his right elbow and both knees were red and ragged. He pressed a hand to his flank.

Kila climbed the chimney to get a better look. She scouted the path and nodded to herself.

Nax? she sent.

Nothing. She hadn't expected a reply. The little gray was very far away.

The next three jumps gained her the top of the public baths. Ragin followed, slower.

"Is there a reason you're trailing after me like my own shadow?" she asked.

"Sens Goolsoy said I was to go everywhere you go. I'm your partner."

"Do you think he meant that to include the sewers?"

The boy blinked a few times. "I doubt he anticipated that, but his instructions were unambiguous. I am to follow you everywhere. We are novitiate partners now."

"Stop saying that." Kila made a face. "I am no novitiate. Never was. But if you plan to follow me, you'll have to keep up."

She set off, taking the roofway. Ragin followed her, falling farther back every minute. Kila knew she could lose him if she chose. Her pains were working themselves out of her muscles now that she was running.

She'd pay for this in the morning—and for days to come—with soreness and stiffness. But for now she was free, and it felt good, even in her thin novitiate's gown.

At Dunne Medow Plaza she was forced to descend to street level.

Nax?

She got a lot of weird looks from passersby as she walked through the plaza, but for different reasons than usual. A couple men made lewd comments about her skirts being tied up. She showed them her pinky and bit her thumb in their direction. They turned red and clamped their hands over their mouths in shock.

She wished she had Cayne. The loss of her father's blade sapped much of the satisfaction of her escape from the Baths.

Ragin caught up with her as she passed through the Harridan Gate.

"Here we meet again," she said, pointing at the very spot she'd robbed him.

Ragin flushed red. "Am I to understand from your behavior that Sens Goolsoy did not extract the vow from you before setting you loose to explore the novitiates' ward?"

"What vow?"

With mock solemnity, Ragin intoned: "I vow upon my honor that I shall watch over my partner, share in her happiness and sorrow, be a shadow to her as she is to me."

Kila snort laughed. "Did you truly make such a vow?"

"I did."

"I didn't. Come along now, shadow of mine. We need clothes."

Once more she sent to Nax. *Where are you?*

The reply was faint and filled with fear. *In darkness.*

20

BRAIN HIM!

The clothes Kila stole did not fit well, which was not unusual. She hated them, hated the feel of another person's clothes on her skin. But to continue in the novitiate's gown was impossible. Typically, she chose trousers too large for her, and her old shirt had been a marvelous—though hideous—quilted frock with pockets sewn inside to carry her coins and stash purses she picked from marks.

She tugged at the new shirt, a simple pull-over with short sleeves and a square neckline. It was a little short, exposing a band of skin when she bent even slightly to one side.

"We've got to hurry," she said, fighting down a shiver as the too-tight trousers hugged her thighs.

"I'm dressing as fast as I can." Ragin had swiped a pair of fine merchant's trousers, which fit his slim body perfectly. The cuffs cinched around his calves, leaving shanks of hairy pale skin exposed.

Kila preferred her pants to drop to her ankles. But the boy's pants she'd appropriated for herself hugged her hips and legs, stopping just below her knees.

Ragin struggled to put his arms in his sleeves. And no wonder, as his back and side were blackened with bruises. His head popped out the top of the shirt. "That is a jaunty costume, Kila Sigh. Most becoming— in a rather roguish way. I never would have guessed you were hiding such curves under your gown." His eyelids were lowered in a particular way that told Kila he was not looking at her face.

"If I had Cayne in my fist, I'd show you a curve you'd not soon forget. Now hurry up."

Kila tried to hide the flush in her cheeks by scrunching her brows and giving him a sneer. Better for him to think she was mad rather than caught wrong-footed by his statement. She wasn't sure if he'd meant it as a compliment or mockery.

Digging her thumbs into her waistband, she gave a fruitless tug to loosen it. "You look like a puff-necked lordling," she groused. Not accurate, but it put him on his heels. She almost regretted saying it, seeing how his face fell. But he was wasting time.

"Can you please explain why the sudden rush?" he asked.

She yanked the bottom of her shirt, wishing it were longer. It would have to do. At least her new frocks were clean. And the deep charcoal color was darker than Nax's fur. Perfect for skulking about in shadows.

"I told you. Finta and my friends are in trouble." And Nax.

He made a sarcastic bow. "Lead on, then."

She gave up making her clothing more comfortable. Leading Ragin the easy way down from the Cherry Bottom Inn irritated her. The young man was strong enough to climb, but his feet seemed to be numb clumps of flesh for all his inability to search out toe-holds.

"What is a Cayne?" he asked once his feet struck cobblestone.

The sewer grate was hidden in an alcove behind the inn. Thankfully it was not raining, or they'd get doused dropping into the sewer below.

"Cayne is my blade. The Sensuals stole it. I intend to recover it once I've saved Finta." And Nax. And Henley.

The grate lifted easily, having been fitted with a counterweight. A rusty iron ladder dropped them the ten paces to the wooden walkway installed by thinnies.

Kila bit her lip, worrying about the situation she'd find in the sewers. Nax being caught and put in a box could mean any number of things. None of them were good. At least the thinnies hadn't eaten her. Yet.

Naxie? Are you still breathing?

Yes.

Has Lop been stuffed in a cage, too?

I do not know.

Have Fallo and Yiqa been snatched up?

I do not know. These people have put me in a dark place. I am thirsty.

Ragin sniffed the air. "Horrendous. Do you frequent this tunnel?"

"If you want to get from Cheapsgate to Terriside, it's this or the Cheaps."

"And the Cheaps is the lesser choice?" He seemed amused by this.

"My face is known to the Watch. And there's the small matter of my little gray friend."

Ragin squinted at her. "Pardon me? Did you say you have a little gray friend?"

"My cat. The one you asked me about. She's gray."

He frowned and scratched his chin. "That filthy creature you stole from me was gray?"

"No." Kila started along the walkway. A few inches of fetid water slicked the bottom of the tunnel. Debris washed from the city streets mixed into a slurry of leaves, atlen feathers, stray bits of clothing, chunks of wood. A child's rag doll floated by.

No matter what one found there, one did not take *anything* from the sewers. If a thinnie caught someone scavenging from the sewer beds . . . Well, they were not a forgiving clan.

This time she didn't head for Cheapsgate. She went deeper under the city. It was all new territory for her.

"I told you before. The creature I *rescued* from you is a creamy white tangleball named Oly. He's about as pleasant as a sober Donse Master with bleeding arse sores. Oly bonded to my brother."

A side tunnel joined to the main tunnel. There were fewer grates on the street above in that direction. But that's where Kila had to go. There were no boardwalks built along the sides.

Stepping off the walkway, she started along the slick moist stone. Goo squelched between her toes. She mostly succeeded at staying out of the standing water. Ragin sucked air through his teeth and made noises of disgust. "How do you go about without shoes? My feet are *shredded*."

"Start by never having shoes, then don't ever put any on."

That shut him up.

"When the thinnies surround us, just be still," she said over her shoulder. "They're a bit loose with their blowpipes."

"Blowpipes?"

She spread her hands apart. "Wood tubes about this long. They put darts in 'em and blow. Sends the little stabber at you fast as a lightning bolt. Never took one in my own hide, but I hear the poison they dab on the barbs stings like a hot poker to the eyeball."

The tunnel ahead lay in shadow, lit farther down by a distant grate on the ceiling. Kila gauged it was three city blocks away. The sound of dripping water resonated in the tunnel. A moldy, rotten taste hung in the air.

If they kept going this direction, she gauged they would pass beneath the Blasted Quarter, a section of Starside filled with ruined buildings. No one lived there. No one could, as the stone foundations were crumbling. Sometimes whole walls sheared off and piled onto the streets below. Those collapses sometimes kicked plumes of dust so high into the air she could see them from Cheapsgate.

As unsafe as the Blasted Quarter was, Kila loved going to the highest buildings and looking out over the city. She believed she knew which ones were safe enough. Wen did not agree.

Something whipped against the hair on the side of her head. A soft click sounded in the tunnel behind her.

"Stop, Ragin," she said.

He kept going, so she grabbed his elbow. "Stop. Someone loosed a warning shot past my head just now."

"Dart?"

"Slingshot, I think. A rock."

Kids in Cheapgate were expert with the simple weapons, often pegging each other with pebbles for sport. Kila never had the patience for them, though she'd made a couple. All it took was two lengths of narrow rope, a leather strap tied between to hold the slingstone, then whirl it about and let fly at just the right moment.

"Do you suggest we wait to be brained?" Ragin said.

He had a point.

Kila raised her hands out to her sides. Time to talk Cheaps. "I'm here t' speak with ya about the ol' lady. Finta Sahng. She's a friend and I just want t' make sure yer not abusin' her."

Nax? Kila sent. *Can you hear my voice where you are?*

No.

Kila had suspected as much. Nax was much farther along in the tunnels. And based on Kila's sense, quite a bit deeper beneath the city than Kila currently was.

Out of habit, she patted her thigh, reaching for Cayne. Not there.

Ragin took a slow step backward. "Perhaps we should retreat and rethink this course of action."

Nax, can you speak with Lop?

No.

Another stone flew past Kila's head, this one ruffling the hair on her right side. Ragin sensed it, too. He ducked.

The warning shots made Kila's skin tingle. She welcomed the feeling, encouraged it. Relaxing her vision, she allowed her mercus vision to show her the metals in the darkness ahead. Stray nails on the sewer floor. A twist of wire. The grate far ahead.

In the blackness, twenty paces directly ahead, two

tiny sparks of gold seemed to hover in mid-air. Earrings. A necklace of silver floated next to it.

Two people.

Belt buckles appeared. Finger rings. Lots of finger rings. Thinnies found such trinkets in the sewers—at least, that's what Wen said. Kila had heard the sewer clan sometimes snatched people from the streets, murdered them, and stole their possessions.

She was relieved to not see daggers or swords. No metal weapons. The blowpipes were wooden.

"The two of ya should stop hurlin' rocks at our heads," she called. "I need to chat with one of you two. If ya please."

A jerk of the earrings showed a bit of startlement that Kila had counted them. Kila took a single step forward, hands still out to her sides. "I promise I won't steal yer earrings or necklace—though it looks to be fine silver."

"What under Til's great sky are you talking about?" Ragin said. His head thrust forward as he tried to duck and peer into the darkness at the same time.

"There are two of 'em just ahead. They're whisperin' to each other."

That gave her an idea. She held her breath and focused her mercus attention on hearing.

". . . kill them both. Our orders were clear." A feminine voice, but steely.

"She knows Finta. Claimed to be the old hag's friend."

"What difference does that make?"

"Fair enough. I'll take the one on the right."

By Kila's reckoning, she was the one on the right. "Follow me," she said to Ragin and sprinted forward.

The two thinnies had not anticipated a direct assault. They backpedaled and crouched.

Even with the zing upon her, Kila smelled them before she saw any hint of their dark clothes and caps. A gamey, muddy smell of people who had not been out in the rain in recent memory. The scuff of their feet on the stone made slick sounds. They wore boots.

The one with the earrings got a gutful of Kila's shoulder. The breath blasted from of the woman's lungs. Her head cracked onto the floor and her body went limp.

The situation was the exact opposite with Ragin. His assailant had gotten on top of him and was raining down blows. Kila cursed and tackled Ragin's attacker.

Kila knew how to immobilize an enemy by twining her arms and legs through theirs just so. In fact, she had used this same hold—arms looping through here, legs squeezing here—on Ragin when she'd robbed him.

Ragin pulled himself off the slimy floor and shook his sodden feet. "Yuck."

"If you're quite finished complaining about the muck, how about helping me with this bloke."

The bloke was a boy—maybe Kila's age. He was small, which made Ragin's failure all the more embarrassing. The lad was also handy with the swear words. Kila increased pressure with her legs until he shut his mouth.

"What's yer name, son?" she said.

"Damn your eyes, villain," the boy said. "I'll have you peeled, diced, and fried before the day is done."

"Feisty one, isn't he?" Ragin said. He'd found a length of wood—a piece of axe handle it looked like. He bounced it in one palm, trying to look menacing. Kila thought he might hit himself by mistake if he wasn't careful. Ragin prodded the boy's exposed stomach with the club. "Answer the question."

The boy relaxed a little, but Kila wasn't going to fall for that trick. She kept her grip on him. "Name?"

"Socky."

"That's a right stupid name," Kila said. "Suits ya well. Now listen to me, Socky. I'm going to let ya free. Yer goin' to keep yer backside planted on the floor until we tell ya to stand, got it?"

"I got it."

"Get ready ta brain him, Ragin."

Ragin hefted the club. In the dimness, his pale hair and complexion gave him a ghostly quality, making him look more dangerous that he would have in broad daylight.

Kila released Socky and sprang up, ready to fight.

The boy stayed put. The woman was still unconscious.

"Now then, where's my cat?"

"What cat? I thought you wanted the old hag." Socky's face was impossible to read in the dimness. Kila wished she knew that mercus light trick Sens Goolsoy had showed her.

"Ragin, can ya make light?"

"Uh, no."

It had been worth a try. She still had her mercus vision going, at least. The boy wore the necklace. Silver. Certainly stolen. He also had a few copper plugs in a pocket. Kila didn't believe his ignorance about her cat. Such animals were rare and word would get around.

"I think ya misunderstood my question," she said, squatting in front of Socky. "I asked ya where my cat is. The only words that ought to be comin' from yer mouth are about where the cat is."

"I told you, I don't know about any cat."

"Conk him on the noggin'," Kila ordered Ragin.

Ragin shifted from foot to foot but didn't raise the club.

"Brain him!" Kila shouted, startling Ragin so bad he backed up a step. Her voice echoed down the tunnel for several seconds after. She snatched the club away from him. Useless boy.

Raising it over her head, she shouted, "One more

chance, Socky."

The boy raised his arms. "I dunno. I dunno. Not exactly, anyway."

Progress. Kila lowered the club. "Ragin. Stay here an' watch this other one. Don't let her wake up and come after me."

"I'm sworn to go where you go," he said. His tone told her the futility of arguing.

"Suit yerself." She shoved the club back into Ragin's hands. "Watch him."

She patted the woman's body and found what she needed. The slingshot was sturdy. She used it to bind the woman's ankles to her wrists. She'd learned a few sailor's knots in her day. The bindings would hold. Further exploration of the woman's clothes turned up a few coins, and a cloth folded over a slice of bread. Kila shoved half the slice in her own mouth. Stale, but good.

Socky got the same shakedown. He had more bread and some smoked fish. Kila divided the provender between her and Ragin.

"Clasp yer hands behind yer back," she ordered Socky. "Ask before you let go of 'em or Ragin'll give yer skull a tickle."

Socky obeyed, though he got in some good swearing under his breath. Kila wondered why he wasn't putting up a greater fight. Maybe she'd frightened him by so easily wrapping him up in a helpless ball.

"Lead us to the cat," she ordered Socky. "Make a break for it, an' I'll knock ya flat and stick yer nose in the slime."

Socky marched down the tunnel.

"Do you really trust him not to lead us into a trap?" Ragin whispered. "There must be many more of these people ahead."

"I don't trust him at all. But I trust how much pain I'll place on his head if he tries anything tricky."

She didn't add that she still held onto her mercus vision. She thought she'd see any thinnies lying in wait ahead of them.

"I noticed you've started calling me Ragin. I appreciate your friendship."

What was it with some people? They had to draw attention to a thing, which only served to ruin the very thing they were shining a light on.

"Saves me some tongue time by clippin' off that last bit of yer name, Ragin*alt*. Don't read too much into it."

He eyed her as they walked. "Have it your way, Stop Thief."

For some reason, his twist of her own joke caused a mental flinch. She somewhat regretted being mean to him. But why couldn't he just keep quiet? There was no purpose in talking about such things.

"Hush," she said. "I need to focus on the dangers ahead of us."

21

TOO SSSTUPIT

The tunnels grew darker as Kila and Raginalt trekked through narrower and narrower sections. The water and debris at the bottom also thinned until the floor was just dusty with a layer of sediment. Finally, a new wooden walkway appeared.

Kila scraped muck from the bottoms of her feet on the edge. "Much better."

Her sense of direction told her they were no longer walking beneath the Blasted Quarter. Socky insisted they were. The grates were few and far between here, and the pieces of the sky she could see were darkening.

"What time did we leave the Baths?" she whispered.

Ragin did not answer. She elbowed him and asked again.

He leaned toward her. "Speak up."

She wrinkled her nose. Ragin apparently didn't have the heightened senses she did. He wasn't in the zing at all. It made her wonder. "Has Goolsoy trained you in the merucus?" She left off the honorific Sens so that Socky wouldn't piece together anything they spoke about.

"Goolsoy? No. He only works with—"

Kila elbowed him in the gut. He grunted.

She yanked on his arm until she could reach his ear. "Shut up about where we're from. I don't want our friend here to know."

"Understood."

"So, you don't have the knack for Goolsoy's training?"

"No. Do you?" His eyes were glimmering dots, but Kila could feel them watching her. Seeing her in an entirely new way.

The denial that sprang to her lips got all tangled up and she couldn't manage to get it started. And that was odd. Lying had never been an obstacle for her. Her silence was confirmation for Ragin.

"That is . . . rather incredible," he said. "I never heard of such—uh, talents—coming from Cheapsgate."

Socky glanced over his shoulder but said nothing. Kila tapped the club in her palm to remind him of what might clunk into his brainpan if he took a wrong step. His hands were still clasped behind him.

The zing was a swarm of sensory stimulation. She felt the tunnel ahead through the sounds drifting to her. Mostly water dripping or the scurry of small rodents. The smell was drier here.

The tunnel forked. Socky took the right branch. The ceiling stepped lower here. The passage ahead narrowed where a wall section had collapsed inward. Rubble lay along the bottom of the tunnel in a mound.

A jumble of stones and timber blocked an opening created by the collapsed wall. Kila guessed a building had fallen in, its weight collapsing the whole structure into its own basements.

Nax? Kila sent.

Darkness. The cat's voice was stronger now. They were getting closer. Kila sensed that Nax was still quite a bit deeper than her current level.

"When will we be headin' down?" she asked Socky.

The boy opened his mouth. He clamped it shut just as quick. Kila suspected he was going to ask how she knew they had to descend.

"Answer me," she said, tapping the boy's head with the club.

He winced and reflexively raised his hands.

"Watch those hands." Kila clunked him. Not too hard. But hard enough to produce a yelp.

His hands clasped behind his back immediately. "Demon spawn," the boy muttered.

So that was it. The lad knew about her connection

to Nax. And he held the same hatred toward it as the Donse Masters. That explained his fear. He was probably worried Kila would place a hex on him or some such nonsense.

The tunnel continued, but Socky turned to a gap in the side. It had been hewn open, leaving jagged rocks all around. An earthy smell wafted through the opening. Kila looked for metals, but saw nothing.

Socky climbed through the opening. Kila and Ragin followed and dropped into a square tunnel beyond. Kila's bare feet sank into a loamy surface, moist as freshly-turned garden soil. It felt good on her feet.

"I don't know where the cat is," Socky said. "If we keep going, we'll run into more of the clan. Don't hit me if we do."

"Take me around 'em. There must be other passages."

"Not at this entrance."

Entrance? She shared a confused look with Ragin. He shrugged.

"So there's no way in without confrontin' more of yer folk?"

"No."

Kila didn't know if the lad was telling the truth or not. Her gut told her he was. And that made things a whole manure-load more complicated. "How many folk are up ahead?"

"Guards at the entrance. Maybe six or seven. Blowpipes."

She had a hard time believing Socky was confessing all this information to her. Was he really that fearful of her?

She sent to Nax, *Have you heard from Lop or Huff yet?*

No.

Kila had to assume that Fallo and Yiqa had been caught. If going farther required Kila and Ragin to pass a guard post, there was no chance they had gotten through undetected. Unless they hadn't tried to go in at all. Fallo was brave and stupid, but he wasn't a total fool. And she doubted Yiqa would sacrifice herself just for Finta Sahng.

Someone is coming, Nax said.

Who?

I don't know her name. She is not gentle.

Let me see.

A wave of panic swept down Kila's back, sent through the connection between cat and girl. Kila swayed as her vision snapped to Nax's. The wire of a cage. It was something you'd keep a chicken in. A white rectangle bloomed in the darkness. A door opening. A silhouetted figure blocked the light as it approached.

A blade glistened in one hand, long and curved.

Fear. Hissing.

The sounds Nax heard came to Kila's mind. "Yes,

hiss and spit," a woman said. "Soon, little beloved of Kil, I will release you from your hateful form. Kil will reward us greatly for it."

The catsight vanished and Kila stumbled into Ragin. He caught her, held her up.

Terror rippled through Kila's mind.

Kila wondered if she could trade Socky for Nax. But there had been something in the woman's voice— a coldness, a ruthlessness. Kila's instinct told her that any threat against Socky would provoke the instant murder of Kila's little gray friend.

"Socky, run ahead and tell yer friends I'm not goin' t' fight."

He looked at her, but his eyes weren't visible in the dimness.

"Go!" she shoved him. He stumbled ahead, then sprinted away.

"Was that wise?" Ragin asked.

"I didn't have a choice. I was given an . . . Ultimatum. And now I gotta turn m'self in. Ya need to retreat right now or they'll take ya with me."

"My vow is my vow."

"I didn't make a vow. Don't count on me jumpin' off a ledge after ya."

"I have absolutely no such illusion, Kila Sigh. You are the epitome of self-interest." He said it with false sweetness that rankled, but Kila didn't want to waste time socking him in the gut. She strode forward, letting the metals ahead show themselves.

There was no warning except for the fluttering sound of loose clothing. A hand clamped around Kila's mouth and hot breath tickled her ear. Ragin kept walking, apparently unaware that Kila had been snatched from beside him.

"You are too ssstupit to liff, Kila Ssigh."

Kila resisted the impulse to elbow her assailant in the stomach, and instead forced her body to relax.

The hand dropped from her mouth. "Well met, Yiqa," Kila said, putting as much sarcasm in it as she could muster. "I was wonderin' when you'd come flippin' in."

The Alnassi woman said nothing, for she was already sneaking ahead and grabbing Ragin. He put up a struggle until Yiqa smashed a fist into his kidney.

Yiqa dragged him back by his ear.

"I have to turn myself over to them, Yiqa," Kila whispered. "They have my cat."

"They will keel you and your ket. Theese folk fear the sspeeerits of kets. Will keel her. Will keel you."

Kila sent to Nax, *Are you still in the cage? Are you hurt?*

No. No.

Where are you?

It's too dark. A box. I'm being carried somewhere.

Tell me when you can see anything.

I will.

Flame burst into existence at Yiqa's fingertips. She

lit a small candle and handed it to Ragin. "Mek yours-self usseful."

He held it. The flames glittered in his eyes. Yiqa's eyes seemed to absorb the flame light.

"How did you do that? You have the mercus?"

"I believe she used a flashtaper," Ragin said. "Mer-cus-imbued strips that burst alight when torn. They're sold at the Cathedral of Til."

"I know what a flashtaper is."

Yiqa pulled a larger fold of paper from inside her black shirt. It was a sketchy map of the tunnels. "I haff fount a way inn thet bypasssses the gaurts." Her slender finger slid from the line signifying the tunnel they were in, to a narrow squiggle starting somewhere behind their current position.

"It issss uncomfortable. But saaffe." With this last assessment Yiqa rocked her hand side to side in the universal gesture of more-or-less. It did not give Kila much confidence.

The map ended in a section of whitespace, a few vague lines drawn in. Yiqa had found a way in, but what lay beyond that point was unknown.

Kila wished she were going alone. Ragin was less than useless when it came to sneaking. But his vow wouldn't permit him to do anything but follow.

She considered hog-tying him, as she had done with the thinnie woman she'd knocked unconscious. The problem with that was the slim likelihood she'd be coming away from this caper alive. Leaving him immobile and at the mercy of the thinnies felt just as wrong as hitting him over the head with a rock.

She jabbed his chest. "Y'll do as as I say or I'll conk yer noggin. Got it?"

"I understand. But a bit of advice, Kila. Beginning your requests with a 'please' would engender more willing cooperation than threats."

"Kil can eat yer willing cooperation for supper. I want blind obediation."

"Obedience."

"That, too."

Yiqa blew out the candle. "Folllow mmmee."

22

ALIVE, OF COURSE

"The, uh, woman is here." The elderly servant's movements sounded stiff, full of disapproval. But of course the man disapproved. He did not trust strangers of any sort coming into the Hargothe's presence. That was as it should be.

The woman stank of worse than unwashed skin. The rasp of her breath betrayed nervous defiance.

"Come forward, woman," the servant said. There were others with him, strong acolytes prepared to answer her slightest wrong twitch.

The Hargothe worked up the energy to speak. "A thinnie in my chamber. What has the world come to?"

"At your invitation." Her voice was low, smooth. The education thinnie's prized so came through in her sharp consonants. "Your man said you had an offer to propose."

"How many of the spark spirits do you have?"

"Pardon?"

"Cats! How many have you captured?"

"Just the one."

A lie? He wasn't sure. The Hargothe listened to the mercusine thrumming across the city. The spark spirits had descended into the sewers. And they had flared with great agitation for a while. Trapped, of course.

"I'm not here to sell it," the woman said.

Grudging admiration seeped into the Hargothe's consciousness. Here was a woman wholly out of her depth, face-to-face with a man only rumored to exist, and yet she stood her ground. She knew what she possessed.

"Perhaps we'll discuss the cat at another time. I'll offer you five hundred gold for Finta Sahng. Alive, of course."

His offer provoked a gasp of shock. Good. She had not been expecting an offer for the Voluptuary's sister. The Hargothe listened even closer, heard the woman's heartbeat. She was here merely to show the minimum tolerable respect. One couldn't refuse an audience with the Hargothe. But she had not foreseen a discussion about ransoming the old woman.

"You hesitate to accept," the Hargothe said.

"She is needed."

The only reason the woman had not accepted his price was that Sahng's skills were more valuable to the thinnies than gold. That meant Sahng was plying her trade, mixing draughts and salves. Someone among the thinnies was ill.

"I might loan you Dunne Yples for a ten-day. Surely you've heard of his skill." A mercus healer of great renown, Dunne Yples attended to the Radiant families of Gristenside.

"I have." The woman was suspicious. His offer likely seemed too generous. Now she wondered why he wanted the old woman so badly.

"I'll not increase my offer. Nor will I offer it again should you leave without accepting."

"I accept."

The elderly servant knew his position. He came forward while the two strong acolytes guided the thinnie woman away.

"See to the arrangements. Lock Finta Sahng in a cell. Instruct Dunne Yples to come to me for additional instructions before descending to the sewers."

"Yes, Seer Hargothe. Is there anything else?"

"Yes. Bring me that new boy you mentioned."

Without another word, the man tiptoed from the room.

23

SHADOWS AGAINST SHADOWS

The Alnassi woman's way around the thinnie entrance was narrow and low. And also filthier than the floor of an alten's roost. The passageway was not a tunnel at all. Merely a series of cracks and crawlspaces and home to a thousand generations of rats.

Something had recently disturbed the denizens, sending them into hiding. Kila didn't fear rats—in fact, she quite liked them roasted—but she didn't like the idea of thousands swarming over her head and shoulders as she crawled through darkness.

Yiqa led the way, slipping through a low space without letting her knees touch the ground, spider-like. Kila had prided herself on her agility, but Yiqa's limbs seemed as bendy as willow branches.

Ragin brought up the rear, cursing softly every time he bumped his head. Which was often. He carried the candle. Kila had thought it odd at first. It seemed Yiqa didn't require light. And Kila didn't either, now that she could relax her senses into the zing whenever she chose. Yiqa had known this. She'd also known that Ragin would need light.

A puff of breeze crossed Kila's face, carrying damp freshness with it. A growing rumble in the ground told of running water, and a waterfall. They came out directly over it.

The plunge of water fell away below her. The air was full of cool mist. But the waterfall was not what drew the curse of awe from Kila's throat. Yiqa had led them to an overlook above a town. A town entirely underground.

Some dwellings were carved into the side of the cavern wall. Still more appeared to be hewn from the bedrock of the floor. The windows glowed with orange light. Street lights stood at the intersections of lanes. They burned with an odd amber light, shedding flickery rays that quickly dwindled into the ever-present shadow pressing from all sides.

Ragin elbowed next to Kila. The shock of the fantastic cavern caused him to drop his candle. It tumbled into the waterfall and disappeared. Yiqa gave him an irritated shake of the head. She muttered something that sounded like "stupitt."

Kila reached out for Nax. *Where are you?*

In a box.

Closing her eyes, Kila raised a hand and pointed in

the direction of her cat. When she opened her eyes, she was pointing straight at the heart of the small town.

"Where is everyone?" Ragin asked.

Nobody knew, so no one answered. But not a single thinnie wandered outside of their stone home. The fact that the town existed at all surprised Kila. Thinnies were disdained even by Cheapsgaters.

"It looks ancient to me," Ragin said. "I don't think the thinnies built this."

"And you deed nyot build Ceetadel or Deevide," Yiqa said. "Humans liiike herrmeet creb."

"I don't see a way down," Kila said. There wasn't so much as an outcropping in the wall stretching down to the subterranean lake.

"Then you arr blind, Kiila Sssigh." Yiqa flashed an evil smile then lunged forward. She arced into open air, tucked, and completed several somersaults as she plummeted. She entered the lake head-first, sending up a tiny spray behind her. Moments later she emerged, raised an arm, and waved for Kila and Ragin to follow.

The boy stiffened and breathed a curse.

Fear sparkled in Kila's stomach. She liked it. "Remember your vow, novitiate." Still grinning, she threw herself into open space.

Her dive was not so elegant as Yiqa's. She entered the water feet-first. Engulfed by a cold as hard as hate, she nearly lost consciousness. Instinct took over, and she stroked for the surface.

She broke into fresh air. A high-pitched cry sounded from above her and was immediately followed by a splash. Ragin came up swearing, tossing his sodden locks to clear them from his eyes.

So there was more to the boy than Kila had first thought. Her father had always said that fear was a strainer. Those who could go through it got through it. Those who couldn't go through got stuck in it.

Breath heaving against the chill, she swam for the shore. Yiqa already stood there, dripping. As Kila sloshed out of the water, the Alnassi woman handed a small vial of black liquid to Kila. Kila sniffed it and winced at the sharp smell of liquor. Worse than Critt Sanglo's trezz.

"Sssmall sseeep. Make bloodt warmm."

Kila obeyed. Only a few drops touched her tongue. She swallowed fire and shuddered with relief as it spread from her belly to her limbs. She expected to see steam rising from her skin as her body flushed.

She handed the vial to Ragin. He took a small sip. Coughed.

He handed the vial back to Yiqa. "What is that?"

Yiqa tucked the vial into the folds of her black shirt. "Sseeecrit."

The mysterious liquor warmed Kila inside, but her skin still tingled with icy gooseflesh. Though Yiqa's clothes dripped like Kila's, she didn't shiver at all. She motioned for Kila to follow and continued away from the shore of the lake. The cavern floor here was dark and strewn with gravel. Behind Kila, Ragin stumbled and cursed as he tripped over larger rocks. Kila still held to the zing. The rocks were shadows against shadows, but she could sense them.

Yiqa didn't possess any mercus ability, but some other power or instinct deftly guided her feet over obstacles in her path.

Now that they were on the floor of the cavern, Kila saw the buildings more clearly. The tall rectangular blocks were separated by narrow alleyways. Perfectly straight. Narrow stairways led from street level to the upper-floor rooms. The only signs of human habitation—aside from the lights and buildings—were the clothing lines stretching high above the alleys. Worn trousers and patched shirts hung from all of them.

Yiqa stopped behind a boulder twice Kila's height. She motioned Kila close. Ragin crowded in, too.

"Your esscaped keptive warned them. No?"

It took Kila a moment to understand. Her *escaped captive*. Kila cursed herself for forgetting Socky. The thinnie boy had surely told the other thinnies that he and his companion had been attacked.

The thinnies were a mysterious people. And rarely seen even in the sewers. But they weren't weak. Just cautious. Maybe Socky had exaggerated how dangerous Kila was.

That made a sort of sense to her. After all, he was a boy bested on his own turf by a Cheapsgate girl. He had to tell them she was as fearsome as the Phantom of Winternight. Kila rather liked that idea.

Yiqa darted from behind the boulder. She led them in a circuit around the fringes of the town. She angled for a promontory accessible by a gentle slope on the far side. It gave them a commanding view of the town.

Nax? Kila sent.

I'm here.

Kila thought she knew which building her cat was in, a structure much like the others, dead center of town. Narrow streets bordered it on all sides. The weird street lamps illuminated every approach, so unless Kila could fly, there was no way to get there undetected.

"Maybe there's a way in underground," Kila said. Ragin started to say something when Yiqa cut him off.

"There." The Alnassi woman pointed. A door had opened on a building close by. Three thinnies came out, escorting a small familiar figure.

The thinnies lead Finta away from town, toward an arched opening in the cavern wall.

"Come," Yiqa commanded. She didn't wait for Kila before slinking away into the shadows.

Kila didn't move. Nax's growing fear buzzed in her mind, her heart. She wanted to shrink into herself, to hide.

"What is it?" Ragin asked. He touched her shoulder.

She shook his hand off. "Let's go get Finta." She

stalked after Yiqa, sick with fury. She hated herself for leaving Nax behind. She hated herself for hesitating to go after Finta. Without the old woman's tincture, Wen would die.

I'll come back for you, she sent to Nax.

Kila and Ragin caught up to Yiqa at the passage-way. The Alnassi woman fixed Kila with a long, unreadable gaze. Kila felt judged and found wanting. Yiqa held a finger to her lips then stepped into the darkness of the passageway.

24

CONTOURS OF HIS THOUGHTS

The Hargothe felt the spark of the boy approaching. The lad was strong in the mercus, but his powers had not yet awakened. The reservoir hummed in him. Oh yes. The spark had ignited somewhere in the deepest reaches of the boy's mind.

The Hargothe's chamber door opened to admit the elderly servant and his two strong acolyte attendants. Between the large men stumbled the boy.

The Hargothe inhaled through his nostrils, tasting the flavor of the boy's breath and sweat in the air. He had been scrubbed, but the stink of Cheapsgate clung to him like a film.

"What is your name, son?" the Hargothe whispered.

The boy said nothing. The Hargothe sensed a stiffness in the air. Defiance. That was good. When the boy's defiance failed, his surrender would be all the sweeter.

"Very well, I shall retrieve your name." The Hargothe sank into the mercusine. To one of his heightened powers the boy's presence was a harmonic overtone amidst the vibrations of power. The boy's mind rang bell-like above the mercus symphony. The Hargothe focused his attention on the silvery ringing.

He brushed inquisitive fingers across the boy's mind, feeling the contours of thoughts. One's name always stood proud among the hills and valleys of a person's mind. One's name was a person's fundamental truth, a fact never questioned.

There it was. He probed it and inspected it. "Pleased to meet you . . . Henley."

The Hargothe heard the saliva in the back of the boy's throat compress as he swallowed. Tooth ground against tooth.

Remarkable strength for a street urchin. Perhaps the lad didn't appreciate the presence in which he stood.

Henley was stronger than the last boy the Hargothe had drained. He beckoned to the two acolytes. They gripped the boy's elbows and dragged him to the edge of the Hargothe's bed.

"You should feel honored to serve Til through me," the Hargothe said.

He lifted his hand, and the elderly acolyte guided it by the wrist until his palm rested upon the boy's hair. Thick, unruly locks.

"And so we begin."

25

VISION TWISTED

The thinnie tunnel began a slow ascent as Kila and her companions left the cavern town behind them. Yiqa made them stay well behind the thinnies escorting Finta. Kila grew impatient. She wanted to rescue the woman and return to collect her cat.

"Why're you going so slow?" Kila hissed at Yiqa.

The woman held up a hand and said nothing. They continued through long stretches of blackness eased only by the filmy light of an occasional lantern. These always marked a narrowing in the passageway where the thinnies had thrown up barricades.

Being scavengers, the thinnies constructed their squeeze points from rotting furniture, shipping crates, and sections of wrought iron fence. Some pieces were so large Kila could not figure out how the thinnies had gotten them here.

The teetering piles of junk narrowed the passage-way, forcing all who passed to go single-file. On each end of these narrowings stood platforms, presumably where thinnies would be stationed as guards.

These posts were vacant now. Kila did not believe it was merely because Socky had escaped to warn them. Something else had drawn the thinnies back to their cavern town.

A sound from far ahead perked Kila's ears. Kila grasped Yiqa's elbow and pulled her to a stop. "Voices."

Yiqa turned to squint into the darkness ahead. But she didn't move. "What do they sssay?"

Kila closed her eyes, focused all of her mercus senses on her hearing. The voices became more distinct, but she couldn't make out what they were saying. She started down the passage, soft footstep following soft footstep.

Without warning her world turned to searing agony, and her vision erupted into flames. Screams resounded in her brain, as loud as a dragon's bellow.

Hands gripped her, pressed her down. She flailed, but failed to fight them off. Something heavy clamped over her lips. A voice rasped into her ear. "What ees eet?"

It was Yiqa. She was on top of Kila. The resounding echo of agony and fear blasted in Kila's mind. As much as it terrified her, it was only in her mind.

Nax pressed her awareness into Kila's mind. *That*

was Henley. Nax was frantic, scrabbling in her tiny prison. *Huff is gone. Huff is gone.*

What's happening, Nax? Kila wanted to curl into a ball and hide under something. But Yiqa still held her down. "Something happened to—"

She cut off, remembering just in time that Yiqa might not know about Henley and Huff. She didn't trust the woman enough to tell her now. "Something happened to my cat. She panicked."

Yiqa climbed off Kila, but it was several moments before Kila could stand. Even then, her knees were weak. A great hollowness made her body feel thin and insubstantial, devoid of all emotion except hopelessness.

What happened to Henley? she sent to Nax.

The answer was swift in coming. But it wasn't in words.

An image of a dark room—as viewed from the floor—flashed into Kila's mind. The vision swung wildly about, stopping momentarily on a figure lying in a bed. The man was as withered as an ancient corpse, his eyelids open to expose empty red sockets. His thin lips were nearly white and pulled back in a grimace that showed black teeth.

The vision twisted toward the ceiling, the walls. It stopped on two men bending over and looking directly into Kila's eyes. They were strong. They wore the robes of acolytes of Til.

The vision faded. Kila sucked in a breath, horrified by the strange vision. She recognized the skeletal man.

"They're moving again," Ragin said, running toward Kila. He came from the tunnel ahead. "Thinnies coming this way. With a Donse Master."

"Ees Feeenta with themmm?" Yiqa asked.

Ragin shook his head. That was all Yiqa needed to know. She took Kila by the hand and led her back through the barricade. She wound through the debris, into a tiny spot where they could hide. They huddled and listened as footsteps sounded in the tunnel, accompanied by voices.

Kila held her breath. Peering through the legs of an overturned bed and chest of drawers, she saw the robes of a Donse Master swishing by. Thinnies accompanied him.

"I assure you," the Donse Master said, "you'll find my skills much more valuable than those of a mystic herbalist. Tell me more about the sickness wracking your—er, settlement." His voice was jammed full of arrogance. He had the long syllables of a man who spent his days in Gristenside.

The thinnies and the Donse Master continued away. Once they were out of view, the three crept from their hiding place. The Alnassi woman no longer held Kila's hand. "Comme. Queeck." With a flutter of her garments, the woman sprinted away. Kila sent to Nax, *We almost have Finta. I'll be back for you soon.*

Hurry. Someone is moving my box.

26

LIKE TWO PHANTOMS

Kila tried to run after Yiqa, but all she could manage was an uneven stagger. Ragin held her arm to keep her upright. Nausea roiled in her gut.

A side cramp stopped Kila. She bent double and brought up a thin stream of vomit. Ragin gathered her hair behind her and rubbed her back. Kila wiped her lips on her sleeve. "Nax is in trouble. I have to help her."

Ragin said nothing. It was too dark to see his face.

"Regretting that vow, aren't you?" she said.

"Less now than before," he said softly.

Kila didn't understand this odd statement, but she didn't have the time to puzzle over it. The cramp in her side had eased. She was feeling stronger. The alivenss of the mercus vision was still with her.

She headed after Yiqa and Finta. A hundred strides

later, the passageway ahead erupted with sharp cracks, grunts, and curses. The sounds ended with a final, prolonged gurgle as someone left the world to join Lumne in her deep, still waters.

Finta's voice came next, a hint of a whisper in the air. "Well met, Bloodsister. Your timing is impeccable."

"*Talle senseenya,* Blootmahter Saahngk."

"I'm well, thank you."

Footsteps approached. Kila recognize the rhythm of Finta's stride. Yiqa's steps were nearly silent. The pair rounded the corner and came into the amber light of one of the thinnie lanterns.

Yiqa's face was blood-splattered. Reading Kila's shocked expression, she swiped her fingers across her brow and looked at the blood with distaste. "Nott mmine."

Finta's wan face looked etched from bedrock, the age lines blackened with shadows from the weird light.

"You'll take Finta to her sister?" Kila asked Yiqa.

Finta started to object but Yiqa cut her off. "Yes."

"Wen is hiding at Critt's Sanglo's dive, Finta. He needs your tincture desperately."

"I will make up a batch for him—as soon as I get back to my shop." She emphasized her destination with a sharp glance at Yiqa.

"Noh. You comme to Betts off Ori. Volupcheweery mek you seff."

"I don't need my sister to make me safe."

Kila took a step back. "I have to get my cat. I have to—"

Yiqa glared at Finta. "Why you preesonner off theenies iff you donn't nneet help?"

"I wasn't a prisoner. I went of my own choice. Once I saw how bad their sickness was, I had to stay. Nine out of ten of them are deathly ill. I was helping them. But then one of them struck a deal to turn me over to the Way of Til. Now, let's go to visit my sister so I can get back to my shop. Kila, are you and your handsome friend coming?"

"No. Nax is back there in the town."

Finta's face hardened. "So. That's what the murmurs were about."

"You mussst commme witt mee," Yiqa said to Kila. "Nnow."

"No. I'm going to get my cat."

With a flourish, the Alnassi produced a small object from her shirt. A needle. The tip glimmered, a tiny droplet of clear liquid swelling from it.

Finta stepped between Kila and Yiqa. *"Parzil connettett, shile."* She held her hand out, clearly demanding Yiqa hand over the needle.

Yiqa snatched the needle away, refusing. In motions too fast for Kila to follow, the old woman blurred through a series of grips and twists on Yiqa's arms until she had Yiqa on the floor, her hand twisted behind her. She plucked the needle from the woman's fingers and gave it a sniff.

"*Filla*. Dangerous."

Ragin let out an inarticulate sound of disbelief. "Did you see what I saw?"

It seemed old Finta could take care of herself.

The healer arched an eyebrow. "I'm older than I look, but still young. Now, Kila, go retrieve your cat. But you must not allow the thinnies to capture you. They will turn you over to the Way of Til, as they planned to do with me just now." She stepped over Yiqa's body. A thin drip of saliva dangled from the Alnassi woman's lips. Her eyes were trying to open.

Finta handed the needle to Kila. "If they capture you, pierce your skin and squeeze. Half for you, half for Nax."

"You want me to kill myself? And Nax?" It was Kila's turn to step away from the old woman.

Finta didn't blink. "If you love Nax, you will. If you value your soul, you will. If the Way of Til claims you, death will become your most ardent wish."

Kila studied the needle. She didn't need the mercus vision to know it was steel. A small bulb on the blunt end held more of the liquid. She pinned it through her shirt so that the tip was safely away from her skin.

"Feenta. You comme to Betts of Ori," Yiqa said, struggling to her feet. "Reechinoolt, come."

"My vow binds me to Kila. I must uphold it."

Finta and Yiqa exchanged a curious glance and then it was Finta who finally said, "Lead the way, Bloodsister."

Like two phantoms, they faded into darkness.

Kila sprinted in the other direction, Ragin trailing after and shouting, "Do you have a plan?"

"Yes."

But not the way Wen would have a plan. She had no choice but to charge ahead and do what she always did. Improvise. Nax's fear was growing again. As Kila ran, she sent, *Show me.*

Her vision went black, forcing her to stop. She was seeing what Nax saw, which was nothing but the inside of the box.

Then she heard what Nax heard. A woman's voice was intoning in a strange language. Her words were muffled, probably due to the box.

And then the language changed to something Kila understood. "It is Kil's wish that every demayne be released. This one has found its way to our world through this vile animal. The demayne has done its part, now we must do ours to release it. Only then can we be rid of this sickness."

Stop sending, Kila sent. *I need to see with my own eyes. I'll be there soon.*

Hurry.

Ignoring the pain and the fear and the hollowness left from Henley's suffering, Kila sprinted. She didn't care about the thinnies up ahead, or the haughty Donse Master.

Her palms itched for Cayne, but her blade was still locked away somewhere with the Sensuals of Ori. No matter. She would break them with her hands. She would gouge out their eyes.

She remembered needle. She would use it on the woman threatening Nax. If they harmed her poor, terrified cat, they'd learn what fury boiled in Kila's heart.

27

PURE ANIMAL TERROR

Two thinnies walked ahead, escorting the Donse Master. They were nearing the opening into the cavern. Kila barely slowed as she wove around the surprised men. She heard Ragin's ragged breathing behind her.

She headed straight for the town. There was no time for stealth. People were emerging from their homes, all dressed in the simple homespun one might expect of any commoner. They shambled arm in arm along the alleyways. Few took notice of her, and those who did said nothing.

Their faces were gaunt and gray. The orange street-lights painted their skin a demonic red, and made their bulging eyes glow like embers. They walked with the heavy steps of exhaustion.

They were all heading to the lake shore. Kila shouldered through the crowd. Few spoke, many coughed.

None seemed well enough to challenge her. Few even noticed her pushing through their midst.

Kila broke into a clear area. There was nothing to distinguish the spot where the thinnies stopped approaching the lake. Perhaps it was fear that kept them from going farther. Perhaps it was respect for the woman standing at the water's edge.

She wore a long cloak of rat pelts. Upon her head, a crown of rat skulls. Lank hair lay upon her shoulders, greasy and gray. A healthy-looking man with strong arms stood next to her, holding a wooden box. Ropes were wound around it, binding several flat rocks to the top and sides.

The rat queen turned to the assembled throng and raised her arms. "I have spoken the words. Kil has heard. We must release his beloved to receive his blessings in return." She turned her face to the ceiling of the great cavern. "Heal us, Despised God!"

She signaled to the man. Kila was already running, screaming for him to stop. If he heard, he didn't care. He spun in place twice, then heaved the box far over the water. It splashed down, floated for a moment, then sank.

Nax's fear shuddered through Kila.

Ragin swore. "They're coming."

Kila stood frozen in the horrific moment. Her skin chilled as Nax sent the feeling of hateful water engulfing her. Kila broke free of the horror and raced for the water's edge.

The rat queen barred her way, backed by her strongman. Kila angled to go around them, but her feet became entangled in some unseen trap. She fell, breath blowing out of her lungs. She scrabbled on the rocks, trying to regain her feet. Frantically, she searched with her hands to discover her ankles were bound by nothing at all.

"Be gentle with her," the Donse Master said.

The man's thinnie escort grabbed Kila's arms and heaved her upright. The rat queen approached from the lake. The Donse Master approached from behind. Ragin stood apart, hemmed in from all sides by the less sickly of the remaining thinnies.

Above all of this was Nax's fear and panic. In short bursts the cat sent her experience to Kila, making her head waver as catsight and her true vision over-lapped. Her breath came in frantic gasps, matching Nax's struggle to keep her nose above the rising water level as water bubbled through the seams of the box.

"We won't need your services, Donse Master," the rat queen said. "I have seen to our cure."

The Donse Master snorted. "Inane witch. I saw your ceremony. Drowning babies again?"

The rat queen laughed. "Nothing so ordinary. I released a beloved of Kil!"

Kila struggled in the men's grip, kicking, cursing. Nax's panic overwhelmed her. She couldn't breathe.

"Let her go!" Ragin shouted. "Can't you see she's suffering?"

Nax!

The cat's reply came through as pure animal terror. There was no air. Just the black cold.

Kila went still, the connection between her and Nax suddenly gone.

28

SOUL-RENDING

I n the atlen barn loft, Fallo leaned against the wall, two cats in his lap. Huff was breathing but wouldn't wake up. Fallo's cat, Lop, licked Huff's fur.

Lop jerked to alertness, fur standing straight out. A mournful mewl warbled from her mouth.

Fallo's eyes squinted shut as a new agony blasted from his cat into his mind.

"Oh, no. Oh, Til, please no."

In Cheapsgate, a feverish Wen sat up in a strange cot in a strange place. It smelled of trezz and the cheap scent of harlots' perfume. Oly hissed and spat. Critt Sanglo burst in. "Stifle yon cat or we'll have—What is it, lad? Yer face be pale as a shark's belly."

"My sister—" He tried to get up, but his weak legs wouldn't support him. A coughing fit came over him and blotted out everything else.

The Hargothe panted where he lay upon his bed. The strain of breaking Henley had sapped what strength he had. The lad should be begging by now, should be pleading for death. Instead, the boy lay on the floor, unconscious, his mind closed to the Hargothe.

It was the bond. The lad had joined minds with a beloved of Kil. Dangerous. But intriguing. The old man seethed with envy.

Henley swirled in a nightmare of fire. His mind threatened to explode. Strange pressures probed at him from *inside* his mind.

A new terror broke through.

Huff?

Nax dies. Soul-rending pain.

Henley's eyes popped open. He sat up.

The gray corpse-like man cocked his head. "Ready for more?"

Henley's throat released his rage. A piercing shriek. The Hargothe recoiled.

Acolytes rushed in and dragged Henley out. They threw him back into the foul-smelling cell and slammed the door. Still he screamed.

29

CURRENTS OF NIGHT

Kila's mind was fire.

Though her eyes squeezed shut, the thinnie cavern sprang into her mind as clearly as if sunlight broke over it. The metal street lights, the nails, the wire. The clasps on every cloak, the silver in the rat queen's necklace hidden beneath her rat pelt cape.

The walls all around were veined with iron and lead and copper. A hidden streak of gold deep in the bedrock gleamed in her consciousness.

She stopped struggling. The thinnies did not loosen their grip on her. The rat queen put her hand under Kila's chin and lifted. Kila opened her eyes, looked deep into the rat queen's head. The pulse of her blood shined bright and red. Iron in the blood.

All around her the thinnies came aglow from the iron in their blood.

A thought slipped loose from some hidden place in Kila's mind. A rage-thought, a hate-thought. It carried upon it vengeance. Goolsoy could make light from a stick.

Kila bent her fury upon the iron in their blood. She ignited the iron in their blood.

The rat queen went first. A gasp released, a puff of smoke burst from the woman's lips. Then her face flamed, her skin melting away. The hands holding Kila released her, leaving burns on her skin. She turned, and everywhere she looked thinnies fell to ash. A red glow lifted from the cavern town and painted the high roof crimson.

Kila's mind was fire. The Donse Master screamed, "Dem Kisk!"

She strode into the water, not feeling the cold. Steam hissed away from her in thick clouds. A voice called after her. Beyond that a scream arose, a chorus of a thousand terrified souls.

Kila dove.

Feeling returned. Not of body, but of heart. She reached for Nax, searching for the tiny soul Kila had come to feel as part of her very own. Now that Nax was absent, Kila felt how much the cat had added to her life.

She swam, deep, and deeper. She knew where to swim. That had to good. It had to be.

There was iron in the blood. She searched ahead, eyes closed. The lake was black even in its shallowest depths. Other creatures lurked here, slithering through the stillness. Kila warned them away with pulses of blood-burning anger.

There! The box. Kila saw the nails. She saw the iron in the blood. *Nax!*

Kila's lungs longed for air, but she would die here with Nax or she would breathe again with Nax in her arms.

The box was bound with rope and Cayne was far away. Her hands found the rope, tugged futilely on the rat queen's knots. The rocks. She felt for the metal in the stones. She found one full of iron. She melted it and the rock shattered. The rope slackened.

Nax!

Still she could not unwind the rope. The nails!

With a thought she pulled them from the wood, sent them flying away in all directions. The box fell to pieces. Kila snagged Nax's fur and drew the tiny gray to her chest.

She kicked for the surface. It was so far away, only a haze of red far above. Bubbles escaped her mouth and taunted her with how easily they rose. Up and up to freedom. Each like a little soul rising to heaven.

Kila kicked.

The mercus sight was fading. The metals no longer glowed. Now there was cold, only cold.

Hush, Kila Sigh. Why won't you die? Why? Why? Why?

We ride on the currents of night. We ride. You and I, we fly and then we die.

Fly above the bells of Starside.

Fly beyond the Divide.

Something pressed against Kila's face. A muffled burbling sound came next.

Fingers pried her lips apart, air seeped in. Then warmth.

"Cough it up, Kila."

Ragin hovered over her. Air surrounded her.

The convulsion doubled her over and water poured from her mouth. She coughed and spat until finally sweet air came into her lungs. Her hands gripped wads of Ragin's shirt.

He was grinning. "Keep your eyes open, thief." He moved away for a moment, then a sodden weight landed on her chest. Her hands went to the fur. Nax.

"She's not breathing," Ragin said.

Kila sat up, hooked her thumbs under the little gray's front legs. The cat's head lolled, the eyes stared at nothing.

The mercus vision slammed back into place, for Kila willed it to. She peered deep into Nax's body. The iron in the blood. It moved still. She pressed her ear to the cat's body, heightened hearing listening for the thump of the heart.

"You must get the water from her lungs," Ragin said.

"How?"

He didn't know. His look of helplessness and pity nearly broke Kila. But she shoved that aside.

She was on her knees now, Nax's body on the stone. She inverted the body, let water run out. But Nax did not pull in a breath.

So this was death.

The thought struck her so hard she wobbled. Ragin caught her, held her.

She longed for sweet death. There could be no life without Nax. She remembered the Alnassi woman's needle. Hands shaking, she pulled it from her pocket. Nax's heart barely beat. The blood barely moved. She held the tip of the needle above her own palm, ready to thrust.

"Don't, Kila. Please." Ragin pressed his hands to her cheeks. Made her look into his eyes. "I will follow you. Even to the grave."

"That's stupid."

"Yes. I do not long for eternal sleep, but to partner you is my vow."

Eternal sleep.

Sleep eternal. Sens Renna's words rose to mind. On an intake of breath, Kila clawed back toward hope. She moved the needle to Nax's body. "Just a drop. Just the tiniest drop."

Plunging her mercus vision into the needle, she pressed the tip to the cat's nose. She felt the droplet pass into the cat's blood.

The heartbeat stopped. *"That which it poisons it preserves. To a point."*

Kila scooped up her cat. "We must run."

Ragin said, "If we can get to the street, we will go quicker."

Kila raced through the town, feet kicking through ash heaps as she went. Memory of what she'd done seeped back to awareness.

No time for that now. No time for anything.

No time.

30

SCHEMES OF THE DESPISED GOD

There was iron in blood.

The Hargothe licked the bloodstained spittle from his lips and struggled to swallow. His lungs rattled as he heaved in a desperate breath. It flowed into him, too hot and thick. There seemed to be nothing in the air to sustain him.

An eruption had shaken the mercusine a few minutes past. The dissonance of it had threatened to shatter the Hargothe's bones. Had he been deep within the thrum, he doubted he would have survived it.

And so close it had been! Within Starside, surely. But no Donse Master or harlot or crone possessed such power. Not all of them combined could focus that much mercus so explosively.

His elderly servant rushed in. By the sound of his wheezes, he had run.

"Seer Hargothe, the Highest comes."

No wonder. Even one as weak as Highest Binel would have felt that mercus blast. It had probably kindled an awakening in a score of sleeping minds spread across the city. The old servant swiped a cool, damp cloth across the Hargothe's brow. "No one will tell me what is amiss."

"There was a disturbance. Those attuned to the mercusine will have terrible headaches for days."

The old servant muttered and fussed with the Hargothe's bedding. "Ah, Seer, you've soiled the bed again."

The Highest stepped through the door. He was flanked by two—no, three—Donse Masters. The Hargothe lacked the strength to brush their minds and pull forth their names. His own stink masked theirs.

"Who enters?" he whispered to his servant.

"The Highest. Nare Wiles, Nare Extemp, and Nare Fillus." He proceeded to clean up the Hargothe's mess.

The three who had vied for the vestments of the highest. Already they sought to challenge young B inel.

"I am relieved to find you well, Seer Hargothe," Binel said. His voice cracked. "I was in my meditation when it happened."

His meditation was a bottle of wine, gauging from the smell that now seeped through the reek.

The Hargothe knew how he appeared to them.

Weak, wasted, a breathing corpse. He could not allow these idiots to see just how weak the mercus eruption had left him. Drawing upon pure will he waved a hand, dismissing the event. "Do not concern yourself with my health, Highest. Your attention must focus on discovering who—or what—wielded such power."

"Was it that great?" Fillus asked. "I confess I felt a headache come on, but I did not notice the cause."

Because Fillus was as sensitive to the mercus as a dead rat was to the crow's beak. Nare Extemp, on the other hand, had surely felt it. But he was saying nothing.

Nare Wiles—who had come up two votes short of the Vestments—had some small facility with the mercus. He said nothing. Skittish as a ground squirrel, that one.

"It was a great disruption," the Hargothe said. "But I received no vision. Til is silent."

"That was more than a disruption," Binel said. "It *hurt*. Am I mistaken that it was full of dark intent?"

"No. Which is why you must send your most sensitive Donse Masters to canvass the city. They must meditate and listen for the source of this power. It may well be a coven."

All three Nares and the elderly servant inhaled sharply at the word. The Hargothe might have smiled at how easily their minds were bent. But he found no humor in it now. "Root them out."

There was no coven, the Hargothe knew. But the

many citizens newly awake to the mercus would be easy to find. And their numbers would support his claim that there *was* a coven. That would bring in more acolytes for him to drain.

Highest Binel said, "Yes, Seer Hargothe. I see the wisdom in your counsel. We shall do as you recommend."

"The girl may be at the center of this," he said. His voice was barely a whisper now. "I sense Kil's fingers at work in the world. She may be his puppet. I *must* have her. I shall pull from her mind the schemes of the Despised God."

"Yes, Seer Hargothe."

The men departed, leaving the Hargothe to gasp and tremble. The elderly servant called for his strong assistants to lift the seer's frail body as he removed the soiled bedding and replaced it with fresh.

So tired was he, the Hargothe asked for tea splashed with hanose oil. That would settle him to sleep and numb him to the mercus for a few hours.

He lay in a half-conscious stupor, body finally releasing the tension of the past hour. First the strange boy, bonded to a Beloved of Kil. Then the eruption. Surely the girl was at the center of it. But she had vanished from the mercusine, as had her spark spirit companion. Perhaps she had immolated herself in that outburst. That would be a pity, indeed.

Until he could confirm her survival, the Hargothe would turn all his attention on the boy. He knew now to probe more carefully. He had his methods, and the protection the beloved one offered the boy would not stand forever. For the pain inflicted upon the boy's body also wracked the creature's. How long could it survive such torture?

The Hargothe intended to find out.

31

NOW, BELOVED ONE

R ain smashed onto the cobblestone streets of Starside. The sound filled Kila's ears like the crash of waves onto shore. The constant attack on all her senses numbed her mind, and the chill sapped all feeling from her fingers. She hugged Nax's limp body to her chest and stumbled after Ragin. Ahead—somewhere in the blurry darkness—a great bell clanged. From the bell tower of Ori.

Exhaustion pulled at Kila's legs and arms. Nax's small body felt like an iron weight in her arms.

"It's just ahead," Ragin said.

Kila climbed the steps. A door creaked open and warm air washed over her. The glow of firelight engulfed her as she stepped out of the rain. She had never been in the Baths of Ori before. This was a public space, where anyone could come to ask the Sensuals for comfort.

The famed Dome of the Gentle Goddess arched overhead, the ceiling covered with a dizzying fresco. The circular hall, bordered by gilded columns, held the three baths: Birth. Breath. Death. The waters were still, lit from below by mercus lights. Braziers burned around the periphery, sending a flickering light along the tapestried walls.

A Sensual sat behind a desk near the door, scribbling notes into a journal. Two novitiates—both young and strong—stood behind her. At Kila's entry, the Sensual stood and set down her quill. "Ori welcomes all who seek her aid."

And she expects to be paid, Kila thought, automatically finishing the truism common in Cheapsgate.

"We are novitiates," Ragin said. His stolen clothes were soaked and clung to his skin. The damp matted his hair, turning it dark.

The Sensual's left brow arched. "Then what are you doing out and about at night?"

"We escaped. But Kila needs help."

Kila's body trembled. Now that they no longer moved, the chill had seeped to her bones. The Sensual saw the cat, took a step back. "Oh, dear."

"We must see the Voluptuary. Now." Ragin went to the woman's desk and rang the glass bell that stood atop it, sending up a jangling chime that made Kila wince. She couldn't let go of the mercus vision, even as exhausted as she was.

"Stop that, boy," the Sensual said. "The Voluptuary

isn't in the habit of granting audiences to rule-breaking novitiates who drag in drowned vermin."

"It's her cat. She needs . . ."

"This is very irregular. Get that horrid beast out of here."

Kila's lips trembled. "Please, Sensual."

A new voice rose in the dome chamber, filling it with command. "Bring her over here. Immediately." The Voluptuary strode in, flanked by Sens Renna and two more Sensuals Kila had never seen before. And Finta.

"We felt it," the Voluptuary said. "We did not know what it signified, but we anticipated that you may need a cot."

Kila didn't know what to feel. She didn't trust the woman, but she needed her help. Nax needed her. She couldn't form a thought, let alone an intelligible word.

Finta rushed forward, hands out. She scooped the cat from Kila's arms. "Drowned." The woman's voice cracked.

"No. I gave her *filla*. I had hoped . . ."

Finta's eyes snapped up. The Voluptuary inhaled a surprised gasp. They both shared a quick glance. Finta gently laid the cat on a side table, stroked her damp fur. She pressed her ear to the cat's body. "Growing cold. Maybe too much *filla*."

Through pure will, Kila focused all of her mercus attention on Nax. She listened, watched, felt the air around the creature. There. The heartbeat, ever so soft, separated by long stillness. Each beat no more than the gentle flap of a butterfly's wings.

"She still lives," Kila said. She offered the only explanation she could form. "Iron in the blood."

Sens Renna folded a blanket around Kila's shoulders and tried to guide her to a cot.

"I must stay with Nax."

"Allow Finta Sahng to do her work, child."

Ragin was speaking to the Voluptuary, explaining what had happened among the thinnies, but leaving out many details. Just that they had tried to drown Nax.

"My bag," Finta said, snapping her fingers.

If Kila hadn't known better, she would have assumed Finta was in charge of the place. The Voluptuary stood back, allowing her sister to work. Two Sensuals rushed forward, one carrying a leather bag. The other a thick towel. Finta wrapped the cat in the towel. She rummaged through her bag and pulled out several vials, jars, and tins of powder. She busied herself mixing ingredients, the whole time talking to herself.

Finally she turned to Kila. "This is the best I can do." Finta had a tiny dab of white cream on the tip of her finger. "A concentration of a very exotic leaf. Taken in a larger dose than this, it would keep a sailor alive and full of vigor for a week without a bite of food. For Nax, we can only allow the vapor to enter her lungs."

"Then it's hopeless," the Voluptuary said. "The cat

hasn't drawn a breath since arriving here. And from what young Raginalt has said, she hasn't drawn a breath for half an hour."

"The *filla* slowed her bodily functions," Finta said. "There is hope still, but she must breathe the vapor."

Kila didn't need to know more. She reached out to Nax, again searching for the touch of the cat's mind inside of hers. But Nax was too deeply asleep, her spirit too far beneath the surface of life.

Kila sensed the Voluptuary's presence beside her. The woman whispered, "This is harder than unlocking the door in the Rose Hall. But I felt what you did among the thinnies. You can do this."

Kila didn't know what she needed to do. When she focused, she could see the iron in Nax's blood. It moved through the cat's veins, ever so slowly. But heating her blood would do no good.

Involuntary flashes of what happened when she heated the rat queen's blood made her sway. She shoved all that aside. An idea sprang to mind. Nax could share her vision and hearing with Kila. She frequently shared the feelings in her body. She did it voluntarily. Kila needed to do those things now. On purpose.

She stopped searching for the feeling of Nax's mind in hers. Now she sought Nax's body. She gently pulled back one of Nax's eyelids, saw the cat's pupil contract against the intrusion of light.

Kila stopped breathing. She stopped thinking.

Instinct had to guide her to do what her thinking mind couldn't grasp. She returned to the subtle world, where the senses touched her mind without the interference of naming. She pressed both hands to the cat's body, imagined her warmth spreading into the animal.

Like a shirt button slipping into a button hole, something in her joined to Nax. A sense of deep calm and emptiness swept through her. Kila hadn't drawn a breath for a minute, maybe two.

"Hold open her eyelids," she whispered to Finta. Her own voice came to her from a great distance.

Kila closed her eyes.

Darkness.

And then light. Kila saw through Nax's eyes. She saw Finta's gnarled knuckles very close. Beyond, the old woman's arms stretched away and away. Her wrinkled face was set in sorrowful pity, lips pressed tight. Every sensation in the cat's body found a home in Kila's. The cold. The pain. The residue of terror.

Kila's heartbeat slowed. Barely coming to her awareness, hands gripped her and held her upright. Someone shouted that she was dying.

Still connected to Nax, Kila's body lifted as Sensuals carried her to a cot. Someone patted her face.

All this was a whisper of a breeze against Kila's awareness. For she resided within Nax, their hearts one.

No separation.

Urgency flooded Kila. Just as she had longed for breath beneath the lake, she longed for it now.

Come, beloved one, Kila sent. *Come with me.*

Kila's body was Nax's body. She inhaled through her nose. Her chest rising. Sweetness streamed into her. The Sensuals gasped. Ragin swore.

"By Ori's loving heart, she did it," the Voluptuary said. "I've never seen such a thing."

Kila continued to breathe with Nax. In and out.

"One more, child," Finta said.

On the next inhale, a spicy aliveness entered Kila's nose. Her eyes popped open, the hairs on her body stood up. She leapt from a cot, not remembering being put on it.

Vigorous chills passed in waves across her skin, while heat blossomed in her chest and throat. She fell backward. Ragin caught her. Her heart slammed against her ribs and her breath heaved. All the exhaustion of her trials had turned to supreme awareness. She hadn't felt so alive since descending from the roof of Ori's bell tower.

"It's the vapor of cicza," Finta said. "Distance yourself from Nax."

Kila had no choice. The jittery insanity of Finta's concoction threatened to send her into convulsions. As she released her close affinity with Nax, the feeling faded.

"She breathes on her own now," Finta said. "She lives."

The cicza rush drained from Kila's limbs, leaving her even more exhausted than before. Someone wrapped an arm around her, held her up. Ragin collected Nax, still bundled in a blanket and a towel. He followed as Sens Renna guided Kila through series of hallways and stairs, back to the novitiates' ward. There, Sens Renna helped Kila undress and put her to bed. Ragin came in, placed Nax in Kila's arms. He smiled at her, bent close, and kissed her cheek.

"Good night, thief."

Kila couldn't answer, for the surface of wakefulness was already far above her.

32

WHO IS DEM-KISK?

Time had no meaning in Henley's cell. Had he been there an hour, a week, an eternity?

Maybe not so long as an eternity. The memory of the living corpse, and the torturous intrusions it had made into Henley's mind, was too fresh.

Henley did not move. He barely felt his arms and legs, all of them long gone numb from the chill and the —he didn't know what to name the explosion that had flashed through his mind.

His breath came in slow waves now. Sounds penetrated the silence, which he had once thought of as absolute. He'd never considered his hearing particularly acute, but he swore he could hear someone talking. Raving.

He'd even tried calling out. That made the mad voice stop for a moment. But only a moment. The endless shouts and mumbles, shrieks and sobs, never completely subsided. And as Henley lived in total darkness, and his sense of smell had been overwhelmed by stink, little else remained for his mind to latch onto but that voice.

He awoke, or he supposed he awoke—there was no way to be certain—to discover he could distinguish the words. The man repeated the same things over and over.

"She is Dem-Kisk. Dem-Kisk! The shatterer. Blood and fire and fire and bone! She is Kil's blood, by Til I swear it. Dem-Kisk. You must listen. Dem-Kisk! She set their blood afire. I live by Til's grace alone. Dem-Kisk."

This went on and on. The monotony of it wore on Henley. He felt the panic building again. He did not want to give into it, did not want to flail against the door until his hands were throbbing and bloody.

"Who is Dem-Kisk? Who?" Henley said, though his voice was so weak he could barely hear it.

But the voice of madness stopped. "Hello?"

"Hello," Henley said. "Who are you?"

"I am Dunne Yples. Won't you listen? She is Dem-Kisk!"

"Who? Who is Dem-Kisk?"

"Kil's daughter. Shatterer. Blood and fire. Fire and Bone. She is Kil's blood. By Til, I swear it. Dem-Kisk. She burned them to ashes. I saw it. I saw. It is not possible, but I saw. Didn't you feel her upon the mercusine? She will melt us all to slag."

Henley screamed for the man to shut up, but he was off on another endless round of his ravings.

Huff! Help me!

Henley felt his cat, far away, but there was no answer.

33

A SUBTLE HUM

Highest Binel sat in the throne-like seat of his position at the head of the Thebkine Table. The council's esteemed servants numbered seven. They sat along the massive wooden table in plush chairs, each attended by acolyte servants whose ears were plugged to prevent them from hearing the proceedings. The table itself was twenty paces long, and stood upon fat legs. An assortment of wines and delectables was set out so the assembled Nares might not pass a moment in hunger or thirst.

The Hargothe was not a member of the Thebkine Table, nor was his presence required by church law. Yet, for the past two hundred years, no Hargothe had been denied a place near the table. In fact, Highest Binel had delayed the meeting until the Hargothe was well enough to attend.

Already, the seer's choice of Highest had paid off.

The young man was under assault by his opponents, and bearing up tolerably.

"The canvass of the city turned up nothing. No coven. That leaves only Kila Sigh, the merculyn the Hargothe has been looking for. If she caused such a disturbance, can we do ought else but kill her?" Nare Wiles was saying. He'd been spouting off for a quarter of an hour about women who used the mercus. "Females are too susceptible to Kil's seductions. Their weak nature and proclivity for wanton behavior makes their mercusine power too dangerous to toy with."

Nare Wiles and Nare Fillus had long been foes. But now they found themselves allies. The bloviating moron Fillus stood and pressed his knuckles onto the holy table. "I move we declare Dem-Kisk on Kila Sigh. That will turn her up within the day."

The Hargothe would have strangled the stupid man with his own hands if he could have reached him. Declare Dem-Kisk and every girl of sixteen would be burned or drowned or slung up by her heels along the Starside wall.

"You suggest *she* fulfills Til's prophecy?" Nare Extemp said. "For to declare Dem-Kisk upon her is saying just that. The people will follow that to its idiotic conclusion. And when nothing comes to pass, it will be us writhing upon stakes in Dunne Medow Plaza."

Wiles leaned forward, his face going red. "Perhaps

you did not feel the chaos she sent through the mercusine, Nare Extemp. But those of us sensitive to the subtle world have still not recovered entirely from the soul-shaking terror her exploits have caused. Forget that she's a mere girl. *Anyone* possessed of such power would be a danger to us, to Her Enlightened Majesty. To Til!"

The Hargothe suppressed the urge to touch all their minds with terror, if only to get them to shut up. Nare Fillus took hold of the dangling thread of Nare Wiles's tirade. "That is why we must declare Dem-Kisk."

The Hargothe had anticipated this lunacy. He had counseled Highest Binel in the appropriate maneuvers.

The young man now spoke. His voice was rather too high for the command his position demanded, but it conveyed the innate arrogance of a man brought up among the rich merchant class. "If we declare Dem-Kisk without consulting Her Enlightened Majesty, we'll find Commander LiTishke of the Watch at our doors with an Order of Arrest."

That shut them up. The Enlightened's dominance over Starside had been a constant frustration for the Way of Til. For a thousand years, the balance of power in the realm had tilted to the Raven Throne's favor. Simply put, she had more men with whipaxes and flickbows than the Donse Masters.

To deny that reality was to deny all sense. Dem-Kisk

could not be declared, in any event. On cue, Highest Binel continued the remarks the Hargothe had prepared for him. "The question of Dem-Kisk is a matter for the Garden. My responsibility is to the people of this city. Declaring Dem-Kisk, without a stronger sign of prophecy, would endanger the flock *and* the Way."

"Then let us hear from Dunne Yples. Was he not present when the girl committed her atrocities?"

The Hargothe had traded Dunne Yples's services to the thinnies in return for Finta Sahng. The man had escaped Kila Sigh's mercusine tirade, but due to his sensitivity to the mercus, the girl's . . . explosion . . . had left him witless. The Highest had wisely kept the man's lunacy a secret.

The Hargothe had visited Yples earlier in the evening. Stripped of his Donse Master's robes and chained in a heretic's cell, the poor man had raved, spittle flying from his lips and smelling foul from soiling himself. The Hargothe doubted the man would ever return to service, though he would provide deep sustenance to the Hargothe. After all, each man must serve Til to the limit of his faculties.

The council continued to argue, but the Hargothe turned his attention away from them. The question of Dem-Kisk was set aside, and that had been his only concern. Now he turned his thoughts to the boy. Henley. He, too, was locked in a cell. The shocks of the Hargothe's intrusions into his mind had left no obvious dementia. Even the girl's flare-up had only temporarily wracked the boy's mind.

That one was strong. Nothing like Kila Sigh, but stronger than most Donse Masters. The Beloved One connected to him gave him strength. That connection was deeply fascinating. Through it, the Hargothe hoped to learn many secrets of the subtle world.

His own body was failing. Time was spinning away from him. But there were ways to gather more days of life to himself. Perhaps years. There were aspects of the mercusine he barely understood. Soon enough he would drain more than vitality from other people. His body need not be a prison cell. Surely there was a way to pull physical strength from others as well as mercusine.

The Hargothe breathed deeply and once more felt along the mercusine for the girl. She had reappeared last night. Her presence had been vague and disturbed. And then she'd disappeared again. The Hargothe was certain the Harlots had her in their temple of earthly weakness. They had certainly seen her potential. The Voluptuary herself was powerful in the mercus. What would she do with the girl? Turn her into a Sensual? Perhaps. The Voluptuary was a schemer. She would try to use the girl's powers to elevate the lesser Goddess Ori to primacy. An affront to Til.

The girl. The girl. The girl. The Hargothe's

thoughts were always bent upon the girl. He merely needed her in his presence for a few moments.

He rang his silver bell, interrupting the Council. His elderly servant was a long time coming. When he arrived, he was out of breath. "Seer?"

"I grow weary. Return me to my chamber. And send for Dunne Marlow."

"Marlow, Seer? Do you not remember his disgrace?"

"I remember all!"

The Hargothe was moved to a small cot, then borne by strong acolytes into the crypts. Once in his quiet chamber, the Hargothe slept.

Dunne Marlow woke him some hours later. "I haven't seen you for an age, Tenn. You look terrible."

The Hargothe did not bother brushing the man's brain with terror. Dunne Marlow had discovered a technique to protect his mind, a trick nobody but the Hargothe knew he possessed. It made him utterly invisible upon the mercusine.

"And I could have happily lived another age without hearing your voice," the Hargothe said. His brother was younger by five years, and hardy. He smelled clean and his breath spoke of fitness of body. He was everything the Hargothe was not.

"You invited me," Marlow said.

The Hargothe had *summoned* Marlow. But he did not correct the hated man. Marlow had always insisted on having the last word. "You've been looking for her, too," the Hargothe said. "Don't deny it. You felt her."

"I have been listening. But you know the mercusine is a muddy swamp for me, brother."

"You know as well as I do that she is with the Harlots. It's intolerable."

Dunne Marlow laughed, high-pitched and long. He did not make any effort to be quiet, either. His noises sent spikes of agony through the Hargothe's skull. "What do you expect me to do about it?" Marlow said.

"You know."

Dunne Marlow's laughter tumbled into silence. Now his weight settled onto the bed next to the Hargothe. The disrespect of such an action would leave any other Donse Master—the Highest included —in penance for a year, assuming they survived the Hargothe's wrath. But this was Marlow and the Hargothe could not touch him. Marlow's breath whistled in his nose as the weight of what the Hargothe asked settled upon him.

"In Til's service, all things are permitted," the Hargothe said.

A long pause. "Til's service, you say? But what you ask is reviled by Til. Isn't that why you ginned up those accusations against me and got me ousted from my position with House Peline?"

"Reviled by Til, yes. That is the doctrine of the Theb. But my source is not so indirect as the cryptic scribblings of trezz-adled women. I live upon the mercusine."

"That is near to blasphemy. Perhaps we should declare Dem-Kisk on this girl and be done with it."

"So, you *were* eavesdropping on the Thebkine Table. Impressive. Given that you accomplished that feat, infiltrating the Harlot's baths should be of no difficulty at all. Surely one of your . . . agents . . . can get in undetected. It collects the girl, turns her over to you, and you bring her to me."

"Surely." Dunne Marlow's weight lifted from the bed. A rustle of robes told of him straightening his garments. "Brother, I dislike being crass. But there's no point in talking around the issue. What—exactly—is in it for me?"

"What do you want? The Vestments of the Highest?"

Dunne Marlow made a rude noise. "And sit in meetings all day? I'd rather open my mind to your mercusine experiments. No. What I want is what I've always wanted. A position within the Citadel."

It could be done. The Hargothe needed only speak to three or four Donse Masters. And to Her Enlightened Majesty. It would cost him little.

"I can practically hear your mind straining over this, brother," Marlow said. "Do you want the girl or not?"

"I do. Bring her to me and you will have your appointment."

Marlow chuckled and sighed. "When you first became Hargothe, I was sure you'd kill me. Why didn't you?"

"You are my brother."

"That's not why."

"True. The reason I don't kill you is the same reason I don't kill my other enemies. I don't *have* to in order to have my way."

This wasn't true, exactly. For one, he did kill his enemies when necessary. He merely saw murder as wasteful. Why kill a man if he could be employed in some useful way against another enemy?

"I'll see what I can do," Dunne Marlow said, and left.

The Hargothe submerged into the mercusine and felt for Kila Sigh. She was there, faintly. A subtle hum among the great vibrations of the subtle world.

If anyone could extract her from the Baths, Marlow could. The man was cunning . . . and willing to dabble in arts forbidden by the Theb. Just like the Hargothe himself.

A SPIDER OR A FLY

Kila and Nax slept for eight days. Both were kept alive by the close supervision of Sens Renna and Ragin. Both swallowed water; both received nourishment through more forcible means.

Kila woke in darkness. A novitiate girl helped her to stand, and without a word exchanged between them helped her to snuggle the still-sleeping Nax in Kila's blanket.

The girl then led Kila by the elbow outside where the autumnal air had turned icy. Only later did Kila wonder what door they had passed through to get outside.

Beyond the novitiate ward, in a courtyard beyond the Rose Hall, was the outdoor bath. Fed by a hot spring, the pool steamed in the pre-dawn chill. A sliver of moon stood high overhead in a sky as crisp as the night air.

The girl guided Kila to the hot pool, then helped her remove her gown. Kila shivered, but did not question why she was being made to stand naked under the stars. The girl urged Kila into the water. It wasn't deep. The hot water burned at first, but once she adjusted, the warmth seeped into her body, relaxing her to her core. She didn't say anything, or think anything. The world came to her unnamed and as it was. There wasn't happiness or sadness. Or fear.

When the sky began to lighten the girl helped Kila out of the water, wrapped her in a thick towel, and returned her to her room. She noticed then that Ragin slept on a cot there. She remembered him saying they were to share a room. That made her think of her brother.

Nax's mind was present in Kila's, but she didn't respond to the emotional probes Kila sent. All that returned to Kila was the great weariness still weighing upon the small gray.

"I need to speak to Finta. My brother . . ."

The girl nodded and motioned for Kila to wait. Kila returned to her cot, gathering Nax into her arms. She slept. When she next awoke, the Voluptuary sat next to her. She had a ring in her fingers. She toyed with it, mind lost in some remote contemplation. She noticed Kila's eyes upon her. "Good afternoon, Kila."

"My brother?"

"Alive. He rests comfortably with his cat. That animal is very . . ."

"The word yer lookin' for is 'mean.'" Her words came out in dry, broken squeaks.

"Yes. Oly is mean. But 'protective' is what I was looking for. And how is your cat?"

"Alive."

"Yes." The Voluptuary put the ring in her pocket and straightened. "We hold initiates prisoner here until they open the door or show us they will always lack the power to do so. This practice is for their own protection. I never thought two of you would risk your necks jumping from the roof."

"I had urgent business elsewhere."

The Voluptuary did not crack a smile. "You are lucky to be alive. What you did is beyond dangerous."

"I jump from rooftop to rooftop every single day."

"I'm not talking about your Kil's-capers on the roofway, child. I'm speaking of your mercus attack against the thinnies." The woman's face was pale, haggard. Kila realized the Voluptuary had not been sleeping much lately.

A flash of memory played in Kila's mind. The rat queen's face melting away. Kila had done that. Somehow. And the others . . . She didn't know how many she'd killed.

"I asked Yiqa to return to the thinnie town to see," the Voluptuary said, as if reading Kila's thoughts. "The piles of ash were where you left them. The survivors are too afraid to move them. They believe a demayne came into this world to destroy them for trying to drown the cat."

Piles of ash. Kila could see them. She remembered running through them when she and Ragin fled the town.

"But we know differently," the old woman said. "And the Spinsters know differently, and surely the Hargothe knows differently."

Kila wondered how the Spinsters—the order of women who served the goddess Pol—could know anything about it at all. As for the latter . . . "What is the Hargothe?"

"The Donse Masters claim he is a seer, a prophet. But in truth, he is merely a man who has a debilitating sensitivity to the mercusine."

Kila remembered now. The watcher. The corpse-like man who'd sent Dunne Skyll after her.

"He may want you dead, Kila. He may merely want you. There are rumors that the Hargothe uses acolytes to keep himself alive. Don't ask me how. I don't know. If he didn't know of you before, he knows of you now." The Voluptuary lifted a hand and turned her palm face-up. Another ring lay in it, this one a turtle shell color. "Put this on."

"What is it?"

"A ring."

Kila laughed through her nose. "I supposed I deserved that. But why are you giving me gifts."

"This is not a gift. It is a loan." She took Kila's hand and slipped the ring onto her finger. "I couldn't put this on you until you were awake. You have to be awake for it or it can do harm."

"Ready for what—Oh!" The mercus vanished, her hearing and smell and sight went dull. In a way, it was a relief. In another, a disappointment.

"The ring is a queller. It blocks you from the mercus while wearing it. You will not be able to use your power, but you also will be invisible to those who look for you upon the mercusine."

Kila took the queller ring off. The mercus returned full force. She slipped the ring back on, deciding that for now it was best to live in a muted world. If nothing else, it would help her get back to sleep. And she was so very tired.

She put her hand on Nax and smoothed the cat's silky fur. "Seems like a valuable trinket."

"I don't want you in the Hargothe's grasp. Even more, I don't want a repetition of your stunt with the thinnies. What exactly did you do?"

Kila looked away, heat and pressure building in her eyes. She had only wanted to save Nax. And while she felt no regret about killing the rat queen, the others . . .

The Voluptuary said, "There were children among the dead."

"Ragin was there. He told you what happened."

"He told me what he saw, but he could not tell me

what you did." The woman leaned close. "Girl, tell me. I can help you."

Kila didn't know what she'd done. Not exactly. "Nax was drowning. I was desperate. The mercus vision was screaming at me. I saw the iron in their blood. I *saw* it. And I remembered Goolsoy showing me light from a stick. I don't know what I did. The iron. I just . . . lit it."

The Voluptuary licked her lips, her eyes ice. "You must train with Goolsoy. He will show you how to control your power. From what you've told me, it is a wonder you didn't turn *yourself* into a pile of ash."

Kila hugged Nax to her and looked away from the woman. "I didn't mean to hurt children."

"Not hurt. Killed." The Voluptuary left, and her departure felt like a rebuke. A deserved one.

With the ring on her finger, she didn't smell the food until the novitiate girl came in bearing a tray. Kila's stomach cramped, and pure animal eagerness shot her upright. Like the starving stray she was, she fed.

Sleepiness returned to her immediately. Nax curled next to her. Sleep came quickly.

She dreamed of a raven and dragon circling the Citadel. One squawked, the other roared. Kila became the raven and flapped to a windowsill in the great fortress's highest tower. Just inside sat a woman of no more than thirty years. Her black hair fell in intricate braids from the crown of her head to her shoulders. She wore only a shift and slippers.

She looked into a mirror, face pale and stark in the dim light of her chamber.

Her eyes shifted and met Kila's. "I've felt you," she said. "Come to me if you can. Bring your Beloved One."

She came to the window and offered Kila a corner of bread. "Now, away with you, dearie. And beware, for upon the web of the mercusine one is either a spider or a fly."

Kila took flight.

Across the city of Starside, people shivered and drew their cloaks more tightly about their shoulders. House mothers closed windows. Grandmothers crossed their fingers and whispered forbidden wards.

Above the Divide soared a black harbinger, the raven.

Why won't you die, Kila Sigh?

Why?

Why?

Why?

The End of *A Raven's Dream*
Book Two of Starside Saga
The story continues in *Mind of Mercusine*.

ALSO BY ERIC KENT EDSTROM

The adventure continues in *Mind of Mercusine*.

Have you gotten your FREE Starside short stories yet? Join Eric Kent Edstrom's newsletter to download the first one immediately: http://bookhip.com/JNPMWX

If you're in the mood for a great YA dystopian series about clones and mind transfer, try *The Scion Chronicles*, now available individually or in a complete boxed set!

The Scion Chronicles